THE
OUTLAW TRAIL

THE OUTLAW TRAIL

BY ROBERT REDFORD

Photography by Jonathan Blair

Grosset & Dunlap • Publishers • New York

A Filmways Company

Designed by Marcia Ben-Eli

Grateful acknowledgment is made to Joyce Warner for permission
to reprint a stanza from "Old Cowboy" by Matt Warner.

The excerpt from *Mountain Man* by Vardis Fisher is reprinted with the
kind permission of Opal Laurel Holmes, publisher, Boise, Idaho.

CONTENTS

For Lola, Shauna, James, and Amy Hart

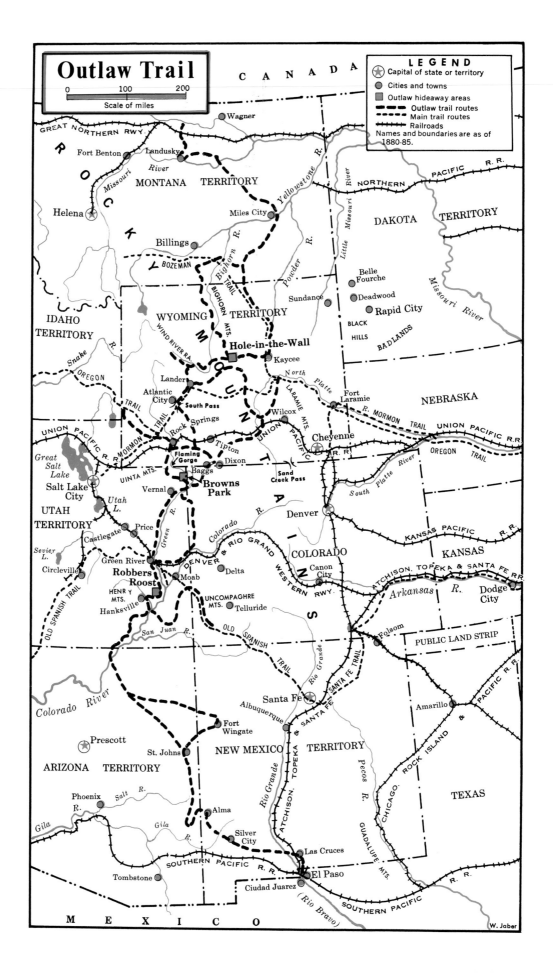

Outlaw Trail

Scale of miles
0   100   200

LEGEND
⭐ Capital of state or territory
● Cities and towns
■ Outlaw hideaway areas
▬ ▬ Outlaw trail routes
- - - Main trail routes
╫╫╫ Railroads
Names and boundaries are as of 1880-85.

CANADA

GREAT NORTHERN RWY.

R
O
C
K

Wagner

Fort Benton   Landusky

Missouri   River

Helena ⭐

MONTANA   TERRITORY

Miles City

Billings

Yellowstone R.

NORTHERN   PACIFIC   R. R.

Little Missouri River

DAKOTA   TERRITORY

BOZEMAN   TRAIL

Bighorn R.

Powder R.

Missouri River

Belle Fourche
Deadwood
Sundance
Rapid City

BLACK HILLS

BADLANDS

IDAHO   TERRITORY

Snake   R.

OREGON   TRAIL

M
O
U
N
T
A
I
N
S

WYOMING   TERRITORY

WIND RIVER RA.

BIGHORN MTS.

Hole-in-the-Wall

Kaycee

North   Platte

LARAMIE MTS.

Fort Laramie

NEBRASKA

Lander

Atlantic City

South Pass

MORMON   TRAIL

Rock Springs

Wilcox

UNION   PACIFIC

R.

Cheyenne

R. R.

MORMON   TRAIL

UNION PACIFIC R. R.

OREGON   TRAIL

Great Salt Lake

UNION PACIFIC R. R.

Tipton

Flaming Gorge

Baggs   Dixon

Browns Park

Sand Creek Pass

South   Platte River

Salt Lake City ⭐

UINTA MTS.

Vernal

Green R.

Denver

KANSAS PACIFIC   R. R.

UTAH   TERRITORY

Utah L.

Price

Colorado   R.

COLORADO

KANSAS

Sevier L.

Castlegate

Green River

DENVER & RIO GRANDE

Delta

Canon City

ATCHISON, TOPEKA & SANTA FE RR.

Circleville

Robbers Roost

Moab

WESTERN RWY.

Arkansas   R.   Dodge City

HENRY MTS.

Hanksville

UNCOMPAGHRE MTS.

Telluride

OLD   SPANISH   TRAIL

San Juan R.

OLD   SPANISH   TRAIL

Rio Grande

Folsom

PUBLIC LAND STRIP

Colorado   River

Santa Fe ⭐

ATCHISON, TOPEKA & SANTA FE TRAIL

Amarillo

CHICAGO, ROCK ISLAND & PACIFIC R. R.

Prescott ⭐

St. Johns

Albuquerque

Fort Wingate

NEW MEXICO   TERRITORY

Rio Grande

Pecos R.

GUADALUPE MTS.

TEXAS

ARIZONA   TERRITORY

Phoenix   Salt   R.

R.

Alma

Gila

Gila   R.

Silver City

Las Cruces

SOUTHERN   PACIFIC   R. R.

Tombstone

El Paso

Ciudad Juarez

SOUTHERN PACIFIC

PACIFIC R. R.

M   E   X   I   C   O

(Rio Bravo)

W. Jaber

FOREWORD

The West today is in a state of change—and siege. Many Westerners are worried about the invasion of their land, space and water. They refer to the coming "rape of the West" and fear the inevitable loss of a life steeped in tradition and custom. Others hope that new industry and development will bring jobs and a higher standard of living. Only time will tell the full story.

But we have already lost much tangible evidence of our heritage: monuments, graves, hideouts, homesteads. Valleys that contained homes and whole pioneer towns have been flooded by dams. Landmarks have been left to wither and die in the gulches remaining after the rivers have dried up or been re-routed for irrigational or industrial use. Bulldozers have destroyed the last remnants of what was not so long ago the Frontier. Trails once traversed by legendary Western characters have been obliterated by concrete and asphalt. Before too long, the only vestige of the West's colorful past may be legend and hearsay.

The Outlaw Trail. It was a name that fascinated me—a geographical anchor in Western folklore. Whether real or imagined, it was a name that, for me, held a kind of magic, a freedom, a mystery. Names tumbled into memory—Jesse James, Bat Masterson, Butch Cassidy, Wyatt Earp, Calamity Jane—echoes from our Western past. I had been told the trail was real, that you could find parts still in existence, if you knew where to look.

The trail itself runs from Canada to Mexico, with the main stem winding down

from the Montana border, across Wyoming, through Utah, Colorado and Arizona, over to New Mexico, down through Texas and, finally, to the Mexican border. From 1870 to 1910 it was a lawless area where any man with a past or a price on his head was free to roam "nameless," provided he was good with a gun, fast on a horse, cleverer than the next man, could run as fast as he could cheat, trusted no one, had eyes in the back of his head and a fool's sense of adventure. No holds were barred on this trail and old age was a freak condition.

Maybe it's having lived so long with science fiction as a culture-mate. Or maybe it's that with our future rush, our need to expand and grow at any cost, we have lost something. Something vital. Something of

Front row: Renée Abbey, Terry Minger, Sherry Arensmeier, Dan Arensmeier. Back row: Ed Abbey, Arlinka Blair, Kim Whitesides, Robert Redford.

The Roma Bar of
Telluride, Colorado.
Below: Arkansas Tom
Jones.

passion and romance. But, perversely, I find
that as technology advances us into the
future with stunning innovations, I become
more interested in the past.

For this reason, I wanted to see for myself
what remained of the Outlaw Trail before it
was too late. I wanted to see it in much the
same way as the outlaws did, by horse and by
foot, and document the adventure with text
and photographs.

The trip was made in October 1975. Eight
people joined in the three-week ride which
was financed by *National Geographic*
magazine. It was a personally rewarding
experience. It is my hope that this book will
make more people aware of what has been
forgotten or lost. To those of us who are
concerned about the shape of our future, the
key may well be in our past.

I would like to express sincere thanks to Tom Smith of the *National Geographic* magazine for his support from the very beginning, to Bette Alexander and Doug Corcoran from Grosset & Dunlap for their ability and their patience, and to Jonathan Blair for his sense of organization and his pictures, which speak for themselves. And special thanks to: Kerry Boren, A.C. Ekker and Outlaw Trails, Inc., Bill Allen and the Allen family, Esther Campbell, Garvin and Curt Taylor and the Taylor family, the people of Kaycee, Wyoming, the Atlantic Mercantile in Atlantic City, Wyoming, Calvin Black and the Hall's Crossing Marina, Lula Betenson and her son Mark, Lois Smith, Barbara Maltby and Robbi Miller.

Hear me my chiefs. I am tired. My heart is sick and sad. From where the sun now stands, I will fight no more forever.

*Chief Joseph at his surrender at the
Battle of the Bearpaw Mountains, Montana,
October 5, 1877*

Why any man would willingly live in a city, with its infernal stinks and noises, he would never know. . . . when he could come West to God's finest sculptures . . . and be his own lord and king and conscience, with no laws except that of the brave and no asylums for crazy men who could no longer look at city life without shrieking and . . . no bible except this land's language for those who could read it. This was the life he loved. And when the hour came, he would be content to let the wolves strip his bones clean and leave them upon this great map of the magnificent.

Mountain Man
Vardis Fisher

The great plains are empty; no more do they ring
With the voice of the old cowboy as he yodels and sings.
Old cowboy, we miss you. Where have you gone?
The old cow range you rode so long
And the old mess wagon where you made your home,
Now stand deserted, forlorn, so alone—Old Cowboy.

From the range forever your voice is still,
No more does its echo resound from the hills—
    Old Cowboy.

Matt Warner
Sheriff of Price, Utah and former outlaw
October 31, 1938

HOLE IN THE WALL

It was mid-October, the transition between the fading glow of summer and the hueless setting-in of winter. When all is shrouded in muted tones: brown, gray and antique yellow. A few aspens struggled to hold their awesome yellows against winter's color drain. It is a time of unpredictability. A freakish time when anything can happen, from a mellow Indian summer to a sudden early storm that leaves bitter temperatures and flushes survival gear from the closet. It is a time to be prepared for anything.

About one fourth of the way along the Outlaw Trail is the small town of Kaycee, Wyoming. The members of our party were to meet there on October 15. I had told them to bring their own bedrolls and whatever personal supplies they might need, but to travel light. Through Kerry Boren arrangements were made to travel in Pony Express fashion—making contact with ranchers along the route who would provide fresh horses and food for each segment of the ride. A four-wheel-drive vehicle was secured to carry photographic equipment and serve as transportation when horses weren't available.

Since the main highways have moved in a different direction,

Outlaws used this wide, fertile valley at
the base of Hole-in-the-Wall to graze
stolen herds of cattle and horses.

most of the trail is obsolete, accessible only
by foot, horse, or in a few cases, four-wheel
drive. I was told I would be met at Kaycee by
a member of a ranching family who would
drive me to a point outside town where the
road stopped. A horse would be there for me
and I was to ride six miles south to the first
camp to pick up food, stock, maps and a
guide. Other members of the party would
join me there.

One of the ranchers' wives, who had never
been out of Wyoming in her thirty-one years
save a brief stay with her husband on an
army post in Texas, met me in a four-wheel
pickup and escorted me to the cutoff point.
She was pretty and tough. Our truck was
slowed by another pickup that occupied the
center of the narrow lane. "Piss-head
hunters," said the young woman, referring
to hunters who drive along slowly, just
before hunting season begins meandering
across both lanes, preoccupied with
scouting the landscape.

The horse was wait-
ing when the truck
dropped me off and I
rode hard to reach the
campsite before dark. It felt good to shake the
city dust from my bones and feel the cold
wind bite me into an alertness I hadn't felt
for months.

As I rode through the wide fertile valley
with the great red cliffs on either side, I saw a

figure on horseback poised on a bluff up
ahead. It was Dan Arensmeier, a member of
our party and one of the early arrivals.
Promptness never having been one of my
virtues, I was the last to arrive at our meeting
place.

I hadn't known Dan Arensmeier before
this trip. I had heard only that he had left
a promising job with the Xerox
Corporation in the East to rediscover his
values as a marketing consultant in Fort
Collins, Colorado. He and his wife, Sherry,
and their two children are examples of a

*Dan Arensmeier galloping across the flats
near Hole-in-the-Wall, Wyoming.*

First night on the trail. Left to right: Dan Arensmeier, Bill Backer, Garvin Taylor, the author, and Kerry Boren.

growing syndrome: young people shifting gears in mid-stride to adopt a different set of values in defiance of the current work ethic. Dan is bright and well-educated. In his late thirties, he has a quick and easy smile and a seeming eagerness to give one the benefit of any doubt. He seemed surprisingly at ease in the saddle and I later found out this was due to his early rearing on a small ranch in Oregon. His wife would be joining us later in the trip.

Together we rode into the campsite, a location called Barnum, a spot just east of the famed Hole-in-the-Wall, an outlaw stronghold that derives its name from a niche in the Great Red Wall of cliffs extending many miles to the south. It was here that the Wild Bunch established one of their three "headquarters" in 1896, although

Valley at the base of Hole-in-the-Wall.

the "Wall" had been a favorite hiding place of outlaws many years before that.

Dan showed me to the camp where an assortment of types milled around a twilight campfire that cast everything in amber and purple. The new faces, old and young alike, were weathered by the elements and framed by sweat-stained Stetsons curled to the owners' liking. The Stetson is the cowboy's mantle, his security blanket, and is doffed only for the rituals of prayer, flag, bed or toilet (and even that is debatable).

Ranged around the campfire were: Garvin Taylor, the barrel-chested, gravel-voiced patriarch of the crew who, at sixty-five, runs the Blue Creek Ranch, some forty acres of which were once a rambling homestead in the middle of the valley; Curt, one of Garvin's three sons, who runs the ranch now; Nicki, his wife, who was to cook for us and who appreciates a good story no matter how salty; Bill Backer, a game warden with not a whole lot to do before deer season, who was curious about our invasion; his wife Nancy, another cook and sourdough expert who also wondered about us; and Rome Taylor, a friend of Curt's and a partner in a bar in town.

And slightly awkward, but no less friendly, were other members of our own party: Jonathan Blair, a freelance photographer on assignment here for *National Geographic* magazine, his wife Arlinka, and Kerry Boren, our historian.

Jonathan seemed electrically wired with enthusiasm for this adventure and had already set up shop for capturing local color: tripods, special gadgets for delayed time reactions, light meters, film cans and a steady chatter.

Arlinka was a pleasant, attractive, strong-featured woman, wearing a mix of Western gear and Middle Eastern bric-a-brac. There was a tentativeness to her, owing largely to her recent return from a harrowing experience on the troubled island of Cyprus.

Kerry's family roots are connected to the Outlaw Trail region and his knowledge of facts and dates was to prove impressive. Smooth skinned, wavy haired, hatless and wearing prescription sunglasses, he was the least Western looking of the group.

As everyone settled in for introductions and filling of cups around the fire, I could see in the distance the famed "Hole" where Garvin would be leading us in the morning. A V-shaped opening at the top of the Red Wall, it looked barely wide enough to allow passage of a horse and rider, let alone a wagon.

Our campsite was on the old "outlaw ranch" where six log cabins had stood in a semicompound similar to a fortress. Unfortunately none are left today. All that remains is one cabin foundation hidden in

the sagebrush where we pitched for the night.

As soon as night fell, so did the temperature, dropping to an unseasonal 30°. Dinner consisted of huge steaks, potatoes, plenty of whiskey for the lionhearted and hot coffee to soothe you into thinking you were warm. There was some talk of the next day's ride and who would ride which horse. Cowboys love their saddle wisdom and pride themselves on looking on any outsider as a "tenderfoot." There followed a brief, sporty exchange about the caliber and disposition of the horses.

Curt: "You can ride the old roan there. She ain't bad, not too hard to catch up if you can throw a rope. She may buck a bit when you first get on her, but not bad. Just make her mind and she'll be all right." (A quick glance up from under the brim to a colleague to share the effect.)

Garvin: "I ain't riding anything if I don't get these goddamned Levi's to loosen up." They were new and starched and his cuffs were rolled up three turns because he wore them so low. Everyone kidded him about it and he said he might have to stand them against a tree in the morning to put them on.

Garvin Taylor is a character, the kind Western literature views with great affection. You treat him with the same respect and interest you would any great artist. A treasure of grit and homilies, you never know when he's serious or testing you

Overleaf: *Outlaw trail riders surveying the approach to the Hole-in-the-Wall.*

or just blowing wind. It doesn't matter. He has such style and humor that you believe everything he says. In his black hat, forehead white and baby-skinned in comparison with the leathered lower half of his face, Taylor's visage resembles a topographical map. His small eyes squint surprise when he speaks—a disarming innocence.

According to Taylor, Hole-in-the-Wall is a place that has its own ways, ways dictated by the outlaws who settled it, and nothing much has changed. "The only way to get here is to be born here," says Garvin, who came to Hole-in-the-Wall as a young boy from Texas with his mom and dad.

Taylor has led a richly varied life and admits to once having been an outlaw himself. He operated the ranch for years with his three sons and then they watched it all dwindle because of rising taxes, land grabs by big corporations, restrictive regulations by the Bureau of Land Management and diminishing profits from raising cows. He views all recent developments with the same spit-on-the-ground attitude most old-timers have—"Things have gone crazy." Riding along one day, he saw some young people hang-gliding off the Red Wall—"Thought they was either crazy or from Mars."

At this point Curt said, "We ought to get Tex down here." "Tex" was Tex Raper, an old saw in his sixties who tends cows for

Members of the famous "super" posse, equipped with horses selected for their speed and stamina. Left to right: George Hiatt, T. T. Kelliher, Jo Lefors, H. Davis, Si Funk, and Jeff Carr.

Garvin some two miles up the creek. Tex, they said, got into some trouble tangling with a bank clerk in San Antonio in 1927 and fled to Hole-in-the-Wall, where he's been ever since—a colorful, unforgettable character.

A short time later Tex rode into camp looking like he had just consumed an entire distillery. With his hat tucked way down on his head so that his eyebrows were barely visible, he staggered to the fire and started right off with rhetoric I thought was to be found only in Zane Grey.

"Howdy, folks. Raper's my name . . . not my game."

Everyone loved Tex. He was obviously the local talent, but was dissuaded from going into town because he couldn't help getting drunk and trying to rearrange the town's layout. Someone mentioned the name of a

man in town.

"He's a good ol' boy—only thing he had agin him was he cracked a few safes. We haven't had a good un since," said Tex.

He rambled off into incoherence, touching his yellow-stained finger to his hat brim and bowing to the ladies in apology for his language, almost toppling over backward in righting himself. He had the amazing balance of one who has stood all night on a binge. Then roaring back into nonstop pure Western raunch with a flow and rhythm befitting the most accomplished poet: "I been down and broke . . . I *am* broke. I've been down, broke and sick and got about four or five hookers in me."

"Or around ya," said Garvin.

Everyone broke up and Tex laughed too and forgot what he was going to say. It didn't matter. Just watching him was enough. He summed up all we had heard or imagined about the old cowhand—rough, colorful, sporty, humorous and valiant, a lover of fun, whiskey and a good story.

Someone said, "Tell about Adam and Eve, Tex."

At this cue the women giggled and turned their backs to the fire. Obviously Tex was a diversion from the monotony of cooking, tending and waiting.

"Tex, you tell the clean part and Garvin,

you tell the dirty parts." Laughter.

"Well, a fella has to be in the right frame of mind first, has to be about three quarts to the wind . . ." Garvin began.

Suddenly, without notice, Tex blurted out the story. Adam and Eve, the how and why. The women laughed the hardest. I missed much of it as his words got lost in his whiskey glass or shirt front. But I appreciated the beautifully paced, undulating rhythm, at once raunchy and delicate—a blend of poetry and porn. He then segued into a deliciously obscene account of "Dangerous Dan McGrew." As often as I had heard it, as much as I cared for it, I had never really known it till then. Tex enjoyed his own stories so much, told them with such contagious reverence, I wondered how Hollywood ever missed him. How many like him are there, were there? Will Rogers is the most recognizable prototype I can recall—spinning a yarn, twirling a rope, winking an eye, and never giving away whether the tale was truth or fiction.

Everyone was mellowed out now, laughed out. The fire, the food and the drink were settling forces. The talk turned to more serious matters. The early days, the hardships, the legend of Hole-in-the-Wall, the joys—the future. Curt Taylor seemed to be the spokesman for the group, and despite a day of wrangling, an extremely cold night and an abundance of Jim Beam, he was most articulate.

"What's happening to the rancher in this area?" I asked.

"Rancher is one of the smallest minorities there is. . . . Goddamned few and gettin' fewer. . . . I'd make more money if I sold and saved on the interest."

"Why don't you?"

"Nothin' short of foreclosin' would pry me out. I love the land, I love this place. It has a fabulous history. I guess I feel part of it, me and my dad. Private corporations are tryin' to buy everyone out. The coal companies and other industries will buy a ranch outside of their coal areas for the mineral rights and trade 'em, but it puts an evaluation on the land so high that some ol' boy makin' his livin' on a bunch of cows—why, the taxes on the land will kill him. Evaluation now is a hundred dollars an acre. If you're out in the boonies and raisin' cows and not makin' a dime, it costs you. You make two-thirds of what it costs you on a cow. There's no way. You're not makin' a damn dime on the land or the cows and you have to pay those taxes. Well, the only thing that keeps these ranchers in business is the raise in land value.

"If someone give you the land and you had the cows, you'd still lose money. For years it was fifteen to twenty dollars an acre. The assessed value comes from tradin', so when the ranchers are forced to take a high price from an oil, gas or electric company, the value automatically increases and so does the temptation to sell. The squeeze play is in motion.

"Used to be ranchin' was so good you could hire twenty to forty men to work a ranch. Now it's no more than five to ten. A lot of jobs for locals have dried up. They either have to leave or go to work in the industrial plants the big corporations have put in. This continues the labor force, but it accelerates the decline of ranchin' as a business. In the old days, some of the bigger ranches had a hundred to a hundred and fifty men workin' 'em. Used to be everyone wanted to cowboy. Nowadays, it's a rare thing. No one wants to get out there and bust their ass, which is what it amounts to. If cattle had gone on a parity with everything else, we'd be all right. They said it didn't happen because the federal government gets the biggest cut. This is a great country, don't get me wrong. I can sit here and cuss the government and somebody ain't gonna come out and get me, but it's like this: Twenty percent of the price of every pound of meat you get in the market goes to the government. I think unionized labor is a good thing but—I mean, a guy who sweeps floors makes more than I do. If government took less of a cut, it might give more back to the rancher and stimulate business."

Bill Backer: "The great federal bureaucracy is what's causin' it all. The BLM [Bureau of Land Management] have more people than we ever did lookin' after this land. They roar up, two men in a vehicle . . . we pack as many as we can in one."

Dan Arensmeier: "Maybe it's the American way of life, I don't know. Casper Weinberger [Secretary of Health, Education, and Welfare in the Ford administration] says that in the last five years federal spending has increased eighty-five percent. This scares the hell out of me."

Rome Taylor: "OSHA [Occupational Safety and Health Administration] is the big thing now. If you want to take a leak you have to have a permit. It's okay to take one— it's *where* you take it."

Bill Backer: "It's come to that."

Curt: "Can you imagine the handbook on that? How to dig your hole, etc!"

Tex: (suddenly alive again) "I don't need no handbook—my life is a dug hole, yes sir."

Curt: "The original concept of Hole-in-the-Wall still stands." (All voice approval.) "If they start takin' away guns, they're gonna have to back me up against a wall and that's no lie. . . . Christ, it's bad. And the water too. They want to get this pipeline into Gillette, take our water here out of the Powder River Basin, and we have territorial rights to that water. Industry has to prove we don't use it—so we make damn sure we do."

It was one A.M. and the speech was slowing down. The temperature had dropped and a light snow was beginning to fall. Some crept away and called it a night, shut off in

sleeping pack, bedroll, tent, what have you. It was cold and the few people still ringing the campfire sounded tired. Only Tex stood—oblivious to all, lost in his memories of legends true and imagined. He sang a short hymn, groping for the lyrics. His whiskey glass was held firmly in one hand like a Colt .45 as though he would keep vigil over the camp with it for the night. I asked Curt where Tex would sleep.

"Don't worry about ol' Tex. He'll work somethin' out when he's ready, or maybe he'll just talk all night. He's done it before—ain't seen this many people in months."

Three of us shared a tent that night. The ground was hard and cold and there seemed to be no way to get warm. I had mistakenly taken my son's sleeping bag and it was too small. I cursed my carelessness as I tried to stuff myself into the bag. I dozed off thinking about the cowboys who spent months like this years ago, when there were no down sleeping bags, hand warmers, snow boots, thermal underwear. I thought about that and about hard ground and hard bones and the saddle for a pillow.

I woke up to the sound of Tex. I had gone to bed to the sound of his voice and woke up to it, like musical accompaniment—except it sounded like a cattle wagon being dragged over a dry river bottom. Someone was cooking eggs.

"Did you know the chicken is the only thing we eat before it's born and after it's dead?" said Tex.

No one knew where or if he had slept. He was in the same position as when we had left him, except that another bottle was empty. He was still cheery and seemed to have stayed warmer than anyone.

Fresh smell of cowboy coffee cut the dead chill of dawn. Then there were sounds of slow awakening—voices, saddle leather creaking, utensils clattering, the sizzle of bacon and sourdough pancakes, stiff body groans and a lot of coughing from the old-timers. Breakfast was nobly prepared by the women over an old irrigation pipe that had been cut in half, a grill welded across the flat space and set on its crescent bottom to catch grease and retain heat. I don't know how good it was—the coffee, the sourdough cakes and the bacon and eggs—but it tasted great. After breakfast all the women except Arlinka Blair returned to Kaycee.

As we saddled up and shuffled our way out for the ride to Hole-in-the-Wall, the morning cold made every movement difficult. Garvin, leading the way, spoke of the Hole-in-the-Wall valley: "This valley in between these great cliffs is where the outlaws grazed their stolen cattle. At times there was as many as four or five hundred people encamped here."

He said it was here they used to plan future

This photograph of Nathan Champion, Al Alison, and Dudley Champion was taken at Hole-in-the-Wall about 1875.

robberies, escape from recent ones and, by many accounts, have a high old time taking target practice and training horses to race and do stunts. Hole-in-the-Wall was one of the three main strongholds used by outlaws in those days. (Brown's Park and Robbers Roost, both in Utah, were the other two.) Garvin said that the Hole was made famous by the Wild Bunch, a gang organized by Butch Cassidy in 1896 and soon established as the most efficient and elusive in the history of the West. "But hell, there was outlaws usin' it years before that."

As we moved along I could see it was going to be a tough day. Many of the party who hadn't ridden in months or years would be at the mercy of Garvin and the ranchers who were at home in a saddle. As I looked back at my companions I could see on their faces what I felt on my own—that paralyzed cold blue around the mouth and nose that cripples speech and coordination. The sky, gray and low, promised no relief. Garvin was more interested in telling us anecdotes than in the weather.

"Right up here is where Bob Smith was shot," he said, pointing to a nondescript spot in a wide field. "Was a near relative of mine . . . bent down to fix a strap on his chaps and they dropped him where he stood. He and his brother Al was ridin' up here to confront Jo Lefors, the U.S. marshal who led a posse into the Hole. Lefors was there with eleven others, and when ol' Bob bent down, they thought he was goin'

for his gun and they shot him."

Garvin turned in his saddle to look over his shoulder at his audience. He was smiling.

"There was over one hundred shots fired, and when the smoke cleared, Bob was layin' there mortally wounded and Al had his thumb shot off and his horse shot from under him. Al ran over that mound there and back to the ranch, which is where we camped last night, and got ahold of some members of the Wild Bunch. They rode up to see what was up but when they got there no one was around 'cept ol' Bob where they'd left him propped up against a tree beggin' for water. They brought him back to the ranch, filled a hat with water and give it to him. He died where we was sleepin' last night."

We talked about the famed Johnson County War where legend has it so many were massacred.

The war took place in 1892 when Nate Champion and his partner Nick Rae were surrounded by over fifty invaders who had been hired by the cattle interests to clean the rustlers and ranchers out of the area.

The invaders had been brought up from Texas under the command of two United States Cavalry majors. Champion and Rae were killed and this in turn brought about reprisals from local citizens and out-

laws alike. The Johnson County group surrounded the invaders and an all-night siege took place. The invaders were rescued by a nearby cavalry unit from Fort McKinney and taken to the fort under arrest. Later, all charges were dropped. I told Garvin I had read a film script that had at least a hundred dead in a violent shoot-out.

"That's a lot of shit . . . only three was hurt. Nate Champion was ambushed in his cabin right over there." He pointed to a flat beneath a distant bluff. "One guy shot himself in the foot and died five days later of gangrene, and another died from somethin' I can't remember. But hell, there was more people shot in a poker game in Gillette."

I asked about Jo Lefors, the famous United States marshal who had practically dedicated his life to breaking up the Wild Bunch and putting them behind bars. He was feared because, like so many lawmen of the time, he tracked outlaws with no great scruples. He was known to frame men, trick them—in fact, use many of the same techniques outlaws themselves favored.

"Oh yeah," Garvin said, "Lefors was somethin'—mean, tricky, seemed to be everywhere. But, by damn, he couldn't break this place. Knew better'n to try. It was no place for the law."

So for twenty-five or thirty years the valley was ruled by outlaws. This didn't stop them from shooting each other from time to time, however.

We were now at the foot of the cliffs where the Hole was and feeling no warmer, though Garvin was smoothly gliding from one anecdote to another. I wondered if storytelling kept him warm.

It was Butch Cassidy who first had the idea for Hole-in-the-Wall, Garvin said. "Patterned it after the Pony Express. Used relay horses stashed with friendly ranchers along the route from a robbery point to one of the way stations, like Hole-in-the-Wall. He's a real hero hereabouts. A lot of the old outlaw characters tied together here. Cassidy, the Sundance Kid, other Wild Bunch members like Harvey Logan, the James brothers, Tom Horn and a lot of 'em. They was all here at one time or another."

We glanced up to the top. Like most legends, it didn't look like much, and it didn't resemble its name. There was neither

a hole in the wall nor anything that impressive, just a steep, broken trail of rubble leading up to a rock mesa. But its appearance was deceptive. It was steeper than it looked and full of loose stone. Tense. It is in a situation like this where horse and rider had better be on the best of terms. Garvin started up without breaking vocal pace. I could feel the trepidation of some of the others behind me and so could the horses. A quarter of the way up, a couple of the horses balked and reared. Leading horses on foot suddenly became the new mode of travel except for Garvin who glided up as though he were on flat ground and seemed to be smiling at the results of the first "tenderfoot test." The photographer, Jonathan Blair, sensing a possible fiasco, or at least some interesting action, scrambled up ahead, cameras dangling and banging against his chest.

Everyone tried to be cool but only Garvin was legitimately unruffled. We got to the top. As with so many experiences involving some danger, the rewards were rich. The view was magnificent and suddenly all the history, the geography, the meaning of Hole-in-the-Wall came together. One could envision how the concept worked. It was at this spot the Outlaw Trail entered the valley. Its penetration in the wall is so small that two men with Winchester rifles could hold off an entire army. Beyond the opening where we stood there was no access to Hole-in-the-Wall from the east. To the west, south and part of the north extended a sea of grassy plains that provided ample grazing for the outlaws' stolen herds. Here the cattle would idle and be fattened on abundant hay and then rebranded for illicit sale elsewhere.

On the way back down I again marveled at Garvin's ease in negotiating the trail. He had never gotten off his horse, and I realized this was simply because he didn't want to walk. Cowboys hate walking; they really know how to use their horses. They conserve the energy of the horse, treating it like a valuable piece of farm equipment. They seldom ride all out, contrary to many dudes' visions of what riding the range is all about. (I remembered the visits of some eastern friends to our ranch in Utah who hadn't ridden much and became frothy with delight when they found they could "gallop." Invariably this ended badly for both rider and horse—the horse lathered in sudden sweat, jangled and ornery, the rider with a sore ass and a false sense of accomplishment.) Cowboying requires real knowledge of a horse and his capabilities. Garvin has it. Curt has it. A horse can sense when a real horseman is in the saddle. He knows when the rider is going to tough it out. There must have been no doubt in Garvin's horse's mind. He never balked.

Arlinka Blair had not spent much time on

Tom Skinner owned the Skinner Hotel and Outfitting Company in Thermopolis, Wyoming. The hotel is said to have housed the Hole-in-the-Wall saloon at one time.

a horse and none at all in the West. I thought her silent bearing under the obvious strain admirable. Her bravery seemed over-whelmed, however, by her husband's voracity as he scampered about snapping shots of everything in sight, from distant vistas to horse nostrils to boot soles to tiny flowers growing from the cracks in the rocks. He was everywhere at once.

The talk turned to wives. Garvin said he had been married a few times. "Last one coulda hunted bear with a toothpick. Jesus, she was somethin'. . . anyone dig spurs in my neck though, I let 'em know it. Didn't last long."

I asked him if he had traveled much. I was surprised to learn he had.

"Hell, I been everywhere. Been to all the states including New York City."

I thought he had a point here. I asked him what he thought of New York.

"Didn't like it—too many elbows in my ribs—I like the space here."

We talked about Tex, who for all I knew was still standing by the coals from last night's fire, talking to himself.

"Ain't he somethin'?" said Garvin. "Sometimes he'll go on like that for thirty days, till he finally runs outta gas or gets tired. Ol' Tex don't give a damn 'bout anything."

I disagreed. He was too much of a poet.

"One time Tex suddenly up and got married. No one could figure it. Tex never was meant for marriage. Had a helluva time. . . . One Christmas we were kidding him about what he was going to get his wife and daughter for Christmas. 'My daughter I don't know,' he said. 'My wife I'm going to get an electric chair.' "

We were down now and riding across the endless flats stretch-ing toward the gray-black horizon. I could feel the strong chill in the wind. I put up my collar and turned down my hat, glad that I had gloves. Garvin rode on gloveless and with only a Levi jacket to protect him, never stopping talking. My mouth was too paralyzed by the chill to even frame a question. As I rode listening to the wind and Garvin rolling on about history, I thought again about the men

Left: *The Hole-in-the-Wall cabin still stands at the foothills of the Red Wall in Wyoming. Below: the cabin as it looked in the 1890s.*

who rode the range like this for months with no relief.

Dan Arensmeier spotted some stray horses let out after the cattle roundup. We all welcomed the opportunity to chase them across the flats, round them up, then chase them again. By now the chill had really settled in our bones so we relished the activity.

Later we came on an old cabin in the middle of a flat that looked like an Andrew Wyeth painting: solitary and sturdy. Small and just fitting for a stop for lunch, it was a relief to step into after the whipping wind outside. The cabin had been used by outlaws as a refuge against the ravaging winds as

The Outlaw Cave, located on the Middle Fork River, offered security and protection to Civil War deserters and later to other men on the run.

they swept across the flat plain. The small wood frame windows rattled threateningly and it was nice to know it had stood for sixty years. Talk turned once again to the threat to the valley.

"An irrigation company wants to dam up part of this whole valley on the Powder River and send water in a line to a power plant a hundred miles away in Gillette," said Curt. "The water rights are to be purchased by oil companies who have a big interest in the plant, so the purchase of water rights would enable them to build the dam. A dam here would wipe out our ranch and a lot of others in this valley. It would probably destroy Hole-in-the-Wall."

He sounded sad and bitter. I thought, there is something unhappy here, something unsettling like a great spirit being broken, and it's upsetting to see. I thought of the great Indian chiefs, like Chief Joseph of the Nez Percé, who made futile stands against the white man's Manifest Destiny and the loss of dignity and spirit they suffered when they were forced to surrender their traditional way of life.

I looked around and noticed that Arlinka and a couple of the others were wearing headbands. I saw the beaded patchwork on her jacket and the leather leggings and I was reminded of the Hopi Indian prophecy that in the fifth generation the Indian will rise up again and the non-Indian will begin to wear the costume of the Indian—headbands, beaded work, and moccasins—and that it will be a time to come together.

Coffee was made, a few songs were sung and for an hour everyone retreated to a personal lunchbreak—napping, resting, reading or just doing nothing.

We walked outside and Garvin pointed to a far edge of the plain where rock peaks stood on the horizon.

"Up there about eight miles is the Outlaw Cave right on the Middle Fork River," he said. "All the outlaws stayed there at one time or another. You have to hike down from some cliffs, cross the river, then hike up to it. You can go—but I'll just watch. I ain't up to no goat's work."

Arlinka, Dan Arensmeier, Kerry Boren and I decided it was worth the trip. We rode to the edge of the cliffs and hiked down a narrow, barely marked trail. Halfway down we could see across to the well-hidden mouth of the cave. Had Kerry Boren not pointed it out, the rest of us would never have seen it.

When we got to the cave, it was less spectacular than I had imagined. But once inside, I was struck by its ghostly aura. History weighed heavily in the silence. Carvings on the wall, the remains of a stretched rawhide tent cover and two pillars of aspen logs weathered by worms and wind—history, echoes. Kerry told us of the cave's inhabitants:

"It was utilized as early as the 1860s by Civil War deserters. It became a popular location for Big Nose George Parrott and his Powder River Gang from 1874 to the mid-1880s. In '78-79 Frank and Jesse James used the cave as a hideout after robbing a Union Pacific train near Carbon, Wyoming, and killing two deputies. Afterward, the

"Big Nose" George Parrott.

Overleaf: *Riding to the Blue Creek Ranch near Kaycee, Wyoming.*

Chief Joseph, leader of the Nez Percé Indians.

cave got a wide reputation among rustlers and became a hideout for traveling members of the Wild Bunch, who wanted security within the security of Hole-in-the-Wall.

"One of 'em, Harvey Logan—whose alias was Kid Curry—escaped from prison in Knoxville, Tennessee, in 1903 and came here and teamed up with another outlaw, Tom Oday. Him and Oday had been together on the famous bank robbery at Belle Fourche, South Dakota. The two of 'em hid out in this cave until they could steal horses from a nearby ranch on the Powder River, six miles from here. They were pursued by deputies from Kaycee.

"Just over the Big Horn Mountains across there, one of the deputies got off a lucky long rifle shot, which severely wounded Logan. Oday snuck into Thermopolis, Wyoming, and got a doctor at gunpoint to come out and tend to Logan. The doctor did so and reported that Logan's wound was so serious he would never recover. But he did recover and, in fact, outlived the doctor who died from a morphine overdose in Casper. Logan recovered so well that he successfully robbed the bank at Cody, Wyoming soon after and eluded another posse."

We sat silently for a while digesting the mix of historic ghosts and the sounds of the rushing stream and the wind. We were brought back to the present on a jarring note: In large letters on the cave wall was scrawled, "Go, Go Jaycees" and "Billy Foreman is a turd."

We climbed back up the hill across from the caves, met the others and rode four or five miles to the Blue Creek Ranch. Garvin wanted to introduce us to his "Ma."

Mrs. Taylor was in her eighties and slowed a bit by a broken hip suffered in a fall the year before. She came out of a shed behind the ranch house where she had been putting away some tools, casting an eager but wary eye on her visitors.

"Come in, come in," she said. "Have some coffee."

She is lively, tough, spirited and sweet. One sensed immediately a pioneer spirit, a type of toughness many of the men don't have—a durable sensibility. There were many relatives gathered around an oil-clothed table in the kitchen and we listened to a symphony of chatter about the valley, Hole-in-the-Wall and the people who came there.

"Most people from around here come from outlaw background—family migrants running away from something or another," Mrs. Taylor told us. "Sometimes they leave under mysterious circumstances. We don't ever ask why. We're proud of it. . . . Don't matter. Ain't much left anyway. The hunters'll be in soon, in their vans and pickups and jeeps from all over— Michigan, Wisconsin, California, Florida even. We make some money while they're here, then there's nothin' all winter—'cept the snow."

" 'Course there's that other thing . . . the cattle killing," Curt Taylor put in.

"What about it?" I asked.

"We don't talk about it much—cattle mutilation—no one knows. Find a dead cow somewhere on the range with just an eye gone, or a lip or an ear. Sometimes it's worse—the testicles, the heart, the stomach—perfectly removed with what looks to be a surgical instrument. No blood—all the blood drained out. No sign of death. No footprints, no markings at all, no clues. Several of 'em all over. Gettin' worse. No one's ever seen it happen."

Silent looks were exchanged between the members of our party. Then there was a brief, awkward silence, until Arlinka asked, "What about the police? Isn't anyone doing anything?"

"FBI's lookin' into it, and state officials and medical people at the university . . . but no one's been able to find anything. It's been goin' on for two years or more in Colorado, Utah, Texas, Montana—all over the West. And it seems to be happenin' more and more."

We suggested some theories such as helicopters, medical quacks, religious or satanic freaks or even government experimentation.

"Naw, doesn't make any sense. No motive. We try not to think about it. . . ."

The subject was left hanging there.

It was time to go. I was given some sourdough starter by Leanna Taylor in answer to my obvious affection for sourdough products. I put it in a plastic food container and placed it in my backpack to be used at the next campsite. We shook hands all around, thanking everyone for their kindness and hospitality. I liked these people and I noted that Mrs. Taylor had a strong handshake.

ATLANTIC CITY

Winter seemed to be on its way prematurely and we wanted to get over toward the Wind River mountain range and Lander, Wyoming before the hunters came. They would be flooding the hills like lemmings in two days and no one was eager to be a moving target for some trigger-happy weekend warrior.

The way down to Casper was hideously marred by an almost freakish mutation in the beautiful yawning expanse of space and plain. From a stretch of simple open beauty we rode over a rise and smack into an oil development, an industrialized hybrid of land and machinery. As far as the eye could see were the slow undulating pump drills, untended, ghostlike, four thousand in all. Drilling and squeaking in the sun like corroded teeter-totters riderless in a barren playground. We were struck by this violation to the landscape—an example of man's rush to develop and then leave for greener things. I thought it harkened back to the gold rush—the early boom towns, the quick pitching of tents, exploration, quick exploitation and rushing on. We've been rushing ever since.

As we drove through the tangled abandon of power lines, oiled

A herd of antelope grazing alongside the barbed edges of an oil development near Casper, Wyoming.

*The Hole-in-the-Wall Saloon
(photographed around the turn of the
century) graced the main street of
Thermopolis, Wyoming for many years.*

roads, pumps and shacks I thought of the
Valley of the Windmills on the island of
Crete where lush orchards of wildflowers
and grasses sway in rhythm to the hundreds
of windmills, where there is only the sound
of the wind, the grass and the wood
squeaking.

The route moved laterally from Casper
and took us west to Shoshone, Riverton,
Thermopolis (where the original bar built by
the Wild Bunch at Hole-in-the-Wall now
stands) and finally to Lander, which is the
base camp, more or less, for rigorous trips
into the Wind River Range. The Wind River
is one of the most exciting ranges in the
Western Hemisphere. Short and shallow in
comparison to the Rockies or Tetons, it has
its own magic. It is one of only two ranges in
America (the High Sierras is the other)

An 1878 photograph of a company of men
marching from Lander, Wyoming.

View of the Wind River Mountains *by J. Schutz.*

where you can find golden trout in cold, high, untroubled lakes.

Lander has much historical significance and it is also the home of a courageous and reputable outdoor newspaper, *High Country News*, which in 1969 was a little-known paper called *Camping News Weekly*. It was bought by an enterprising rancher named Tom Bell who had a strong interest in the future of the area. He struggled through much financial hardship and controversy to bring about an environmental awareness with his paper. It wasn't easy.

In 1973 the staff of the paper worked for weeks with no wages. There was no money to pay them. It is said that Tom himself put $30,000 into the paper after selling his family ranch and moving into town. In 1972 and 1973 he drew only $900 in salary. Finally, the *News* put out what it said was its last issue, barring a miracle. In it was an appeal to every subscriber to send in $30 so the paper could continue. Many people did just that, and in one month the *News* gained 161 new subscriptions and $7000 in contributions. This miraculous recovery was reported by other papers in the West and today the *News* is still in circulation.

Just outside of Lander on the climb up to the point that marks the Continental Divide is a small forgotten town called Atlantic City, not to be confused with the Eastern boardwalk resort of "Monopoly" fame. It was here that we had agreed to hook up with Terry Minger, another member of our party.

Atlantic City, Wyoming, is an old mining town seven miles off the main route. A slightly marked dirt road leads into a cup of a valley where to our amazement everything seemed to have been preserved as in an old tintype. A few cabins stood like wooden sentries against stark, brown-and-white slopes. It was a chilly day and we knew the antelope season was on. We could hear the occasional ricochet of thunder from a 12-gauge shotgun off in the hills.

There is only one hub of activity in Atlantic City. It is the Mercantile, a combination bar and general store where one can get any supplies needed to survive or thrive. Here one is instantly cast back to the era of suspendered store clerks with rumpled cowboy hats, high collars, moustaches and haircuts that left the ears naked (and quite a bit of scalp around them) and the wide-eyed stares of people who looked on a camera as some crazy new invention.

We went inside and there at the bar was Terry Minger. He had been waiting for us for hours and was probably thinking all this was a great put-on. Terry is the town manager of Vail, Colorado, a stocky bearded man in his early thirties with an obvious taste for adventure. He had been told to show up in Atlantic City on October 16 and wait in the bar. I acknowledged his sense of sport in following such sketchy directions. I thought if all town managers were so adventurous they would probably learn a great deal more than they do following programmed procedures.

The old, dark-wooded, original bar has a huge oval-shaped mirror behind it that makes hiding impossible and drinking social. A potbellied stove is the main source of warmth, unless one sits by the south-facing window on a sunny day. The room is ambered by antique glass smoked with dirt and age. On the walls are old maps of Pony Express trails from 1858 to 1861; a January, 1917, Stock Growers' Mercantile calendar; a poster for the Western Hide and Fur Co.; a picture of an old man playing a fiddle captioned, "Too old to diddle, have to jes' fiddle"; another calendar (Smoke El Massey Cigars, Salt Lake City); a lot of documents of gold mines and claims and other such memorabilia. An occasional modern slogan or two crops up, but, essentially, it is as it was.

Terry Wehrman, shy and gentle, is a young transplant from the East who tends bar and acts as all-around City Councilman for Atlantic City. Barkeep, mailman, cook, father confessor, keeper of the good will, he is one of the many young men and women who have turned their backs on the shopping-center mentality of modern city planning to strike out on their own. Sick of land and air pollution, sick at heart at having no voice in where we are going, they, like their migrant predecessors the Linkhorns, the Okies, the Mormons and other early settlers, are starting out from scratch.

Whatever trepidation Minger had felt upon arriving at this strange oasis was dissolving in the wake of the several beers he had had while waiting. Only one awkwardness remained. His hat. He looked as if he had been clipped by some sidewalk vendor in a New York curio arcade. I told him he would have to break in the hat or lose it. He apologized for not looking like a Marlboro ad and said, "Gee, I wish I had a swell hat like yours." While we traded hat insults Jonathan Blair covered the bar with rapid camera shots like a machine-gun strafer. I noticed that he conspicuously avoided any shots of Terry Minger's hat.

At first it seemed hard to get any of the locals to talk. In spite of the geniality, there was that distinct skepticism one always finds when traveling through small towns in rural America. It's a gentle straight-arm against intrusion, a protection against more sophisticated strangers who ask too much, want to get too close.

Arensmeier commented on how peaceful it seemed here, how low key. "I feel comfortable," he said.

"You see," Wehrman offered, "the good thing about Atlantic City is it's a ghost town and no one wants it. Lifestyle here is good 'cause it has attracted the good people, young ones who don't want to work for anybody but are willing to work for themselves, to build something for themselves."

"How do the older folks feel about it?" I asked Wehrman.

"Good. At first, they were a little nervous, skeptical. There aren't many folks here period, you know, and I'm sure they were worried. Thought maybe there was a commune starting up or something. Well, they saw it was a commune in a sense, but one in which everyone did their own thing, but when needed, we would help each other. The older folks have come to like us and feel at one with us. Everything is cool. We learn from them—hints, ways to live, to conserve, to build with your hands, handle the weather and the elements—and we give them help. No one talks about it, it's just the way it is, and that's okay."

Yes, I thought. Why discuss or analyze something that's working.

"Only time we have trouble is when some outsiders come here from the bigger areas. We get fights and broken stuff. It's no good. You ought to talk to John over there. He's built his own house and wind generator for

Terry Minger.

under a hundred dollars."

John was John Mionczynski, a tall lean young guy who was setting up musical instrument stands in the back. He had a small band that played weekends called "the Buffalo Chips." He had a nagging cough that he said was walking pneumonia, which he attributed to getting run down while putting his cabin in shape for winter. Like Terry Wehrman, he had a politely skeptical manner but conveyed a soundness that belied the stereotyped image of the sixties dropout. He wasn't looking to share a

philosophy, he said. If there was any sharing to be done it would be out of genuine need and friendship.

"Just want to make my own way. Don't want to burn anything down either," he said. "Just get on and do it my way and have some good friends, not many, but a few, and learn a few things."

When I told him I was interested in his house he fervently declared that he didn't want any special attention given his house and he didn't want to be classified as a representative of any "new wave." But my interest persisted. I told him I was trying to build my own home using a solar installation for space heating. I also planned wind generation to back up if not replace the need for electric power. He studied me for a moment and then said, "Why don't you come out to my place later? I'll show you what I'm doing." He then joined us for a beer and asked, nodding toward the bar, "Have you met Larry?"

Martha Jane Burke, better known as Calamity Jane.

There, along with three other locals in Pendleton woolen shirts, suspenders, overalls and hunter caps, was an old-timer named Larry Roupe. He sounded like a frog with laryngitis. I went over and asked if I could buy him a beer. He turned a jaundiced squint at me, cocked his head and said, "Who the hell are ya?"

I told him I was someone just passing through who loved the area, particularly its history, and wanted to know more.

"Sure you can buy me one."

The release cue seemed to be that I wanted to listen to him. People do love to talk—most of them.

Larry Roupe and I sat down at a table by the window. The late afternoon light showed him to be leathered, wrinkled and toothless, which gave his mouth a rubbery look. His lips were cracked and stained brown from either dried coffee or wine. His eyes were green and alive beneath coal-black bushy eyebrows. He wore a black hat and rubbed his chin with his thumb and index finger a lot. I asked him where he was from and how he had got here.

"I came in on the Immigrant Trail, or the Oregon Trail. There are two branches. One goes between Walcott, Wyoming and Saratoga, the other branch cut up from Sweetwater to Soulton Pass and on over to

Bridger, Wyoming. Them Mormons was jes' headin' up that pass when they froze here."

"What happened?" I asked.

"Well, it was them pushcart Mormons." (Mormons who walked behind wagons and pushed handcarts all the way from Navoo, Illinois, during their great pioneer trek.) "It was in September."

"Of what year?"

"Hell, I don't remember what year. It's down the road on a marker—you can still see it. . . . A lot of people wonder how you could freeze to death in September. But if you live here, you know. Early storm can come and catch ya. And it can come after the prettiest warm day. It was—I can't remember if it was after the Civil War or before."

Roupe told me he had come here from Oregon in 1922 in a wagon with his dad, who was a cattle buyer. "He'd go down to Texas, buy some big steers for two dollars a head, then bring 'em up to Wyoming and sell them. I was jes' a kid then, but I loved this country. I ran cattle for a while, then took to rodeoin'."

"Were you ever an outlaw?"

"No . . . no, I never went that way. Could've . . . could've been a damn good outlaw. But I jes' never went that way. No reason."

"There were a lot around these parts, weren't there?"

"Oh yeah, all over. It was mostly the way then."

"Even in 1922?"

"Hell, yes. Later'n that. I could tell you stories . . ."

"What about Butch Cassidy?"

Atlantic City, Wyoming in 1903. Mining interests gave birth to this town, but soon withered away and the town's growth was arrested. (See pages 62–63 for a contemporary view of Atlantic City.)

"He was the best. Smartest. Know how he got the name Butch? Worked in a butcher shop over in Rock Springs . . . nicknamed him 'Butch.' His real name was Parker."

"Yes," I said, "I know. Robert Leroy Parker."

"Yeah." He seemed surprised I knew. "Leroy Parker. . . . Ya know, Butch and his boys hung out mostly over roun' Baggs and Dixon, Wyoming. Still a few ol'-timers over there could tell you a lot. Butch never caused real trouble. Oh, a little maybe—they'd turn their horses into the ranchers' pastures but the ranchers never bothered 'em. They all liked Butch. He was good to them. They hung out in Brown's Park a lot too, ya know."

I started to tell him about being over in the Outlaw Cave but he didn't pay much attention. He is nearly seventy and set in his ways, has his own vision and version of things. About the only thing it did was get him to talk more.

"The real bad one was Harvey Logan. He was a bad ass. There was three Logan brothers from Montana. Harvey used the alias Kid Curry. Killed Ol' Man Pike up there in Montana, then he robbed this train down on the Wilcox. Butch and Sundance weren't in on that one."

I noticed that Larry assumed you knew

where and what these names and places were, as if they were all common knowledge. The small world of the cowboy. Later, in checking some of these facts, Kerry Boren found that there were actually four brothers, and that though they came down from Montana, they had been born in Kentucky. One brother died from pneumonia in Steamboat Springs, Colorado. Another was blasted from his horse by a shotgun in the hands of a Montana rancher, who was in turn killed by Harvey Logan a few years later. The third brother was shot down at his aunt's home in Missouri. "Ol' Man Pike" was Parvell "Pike" Landusky, who was shot in the back by Logan in Jew Jake's saloon in Landusky.

"Why were there so many outlaws in this country then?"

"Well, there was gold in the country and it was easy to rob a stagecoach goin' up a grade, then ride on it and hold up the train on the way up the pass. . . . Logan was a mean son-of-a-bitch—jes' as soon kill ya as look at ya. They said he beat the engineer over the head with a six-shooter. . . . He was somethin'."

I asked him what was the farthest he had traveled away from home.

"Oh, Australia, Spain."

Larry Roupe.

"What did you go to Spain for?"

"Oh, jes' goofin' around." His voice trailed off; a mild fixed stare on some unseen object. "That was years ago."

There was such a nostalgic finality to the way he said this that it made me realize some memories are best left untapped.

"What do you think about what's happened to Atlantic City?"

"Oh it's nothin' now. Just a ghost town, lad. And, ya know"—he leaned forward here and his voice became conspiratorial as he shot a look at the bar where the "new pioneers" stood talking with our group of "invaders"—"people jump on that a lot around here, ya know. They try and make it into somethin'. Over in Lander, they even advertise it and all. But it's jes' . . . it's all jes' a bunch of goof! But then, hell, you might think this is jes' a lot of crap."

No, I told him, I was interested in what was really happening. I was worried that we were losing too much of what was good, too much historical stuff. Things were getting blown out of proportion today, we were making too much out of the wrong things.

He leaned forward again, his eyes widening eagerly. "Now you're talkin' sense. They goof everything up here, like this wildlife and all that crap. These

Typical street scene in Lander, Wyoming at the turn of the century.

Below: *Abandoned homestead outside of Atlantic City, Wyoming.*

mountains are gonna be here when lots more generations have come and long gone. I'm an old man. These mountains aren't gonna change—why don't they leave it alone? You take the Forest Service and all them bunch. There's a world of game here . . . of course, you can't turn the people loose on it 'cause they'd destroy it pretty damn quick. But this game is gonna be done away with naturally. The elk are practically gone, the deer too. The buffalo are gone 'cept what the government has saved. See folks don't know how to use it no more, people in fancy contraptions pushin' in all over, tryin' to hunt somethin' to hang on a wall, and

In 1868 Asa Moore, Con Wager, and Big Ed Wilson were tried, convicted, and hanged by a vigilante group in Laramie, Wyoming.

the government boys runnin' around sayin'—'don't do this and don't do that.' There's enough for everybody if people would jes' hunt what they need to eat and the government would back off some. But so many people goofin', no respect.

"Ya know, these mountains was full of old minin' towns. Some people don't know where they're at. Like over at Indian Cabin Copper Mine—that was the largest tramway in the world, they claimed. Don't know if anything's left now."

"What about Anaconda?"

"Been here as long as I can remember."

"Was this a ghost town when you came here?"

"Nothin' was here. All these ol' minin' towns was finished by then. Why, you can go into the mountains here—like Battle Creek, that ol' Victorian minin' town . . . used to be homes there looked like they was right out of old English postcards. Why, I could show you ol' cabins that have rotted down or fallen down. No one knows them, they're all off the beaten road. There are some white man has never seen. A lot are gone that were there. It's all rottin' fast."

"Anything being done about it?"

"Naw. No one gives a damn. Everybody's too interested in development. New timber has growed up around a lot of these old spots. You take Ute Pass. Last time I was in there—'bout thirty-five years ago—everything had fallen down but the jail. And some bottles. Hell, I remember there was three saloons there once—all gone now. Probably ain't nothin' there today but the wind and a bunch of squirrels."

He was really rolling now. He started to tell a story, then got shy of it and said I wouldn't want to hear it. I assured him I did and encouraged him to continue. He looked around again, lowered his voice, cocked the corner of his eye on the ladies at the bar.

"Well, this ol' rover I play cards with, he

The snow-covered grave of Powell "Pike" Landusky, who met a violent death at the hands of Harvey Logan.

tol' me a story 'bout this fella who was always practicin' his fast draw." He paused. More glancing around. I urged him on. "Well, one day he was out takin' a leak, ya know, and decided to try his fast draw, so he pulls out his gun. It goes off and shoots the head of his dick off. He looks down and says, 'Well, ol' buddy, we've had a lot of fist fights, but I never did think I'd draw on ya.' He wheezed a mighty laugh that turned into a throaty cough before it was done. "Ain't that somethin'?" he roared, pleased with himself. I acknowledged that it was.

"**N**ow I could tell ya things about this country no one knows if we got down to business. Things like the 'Big Die Up.' That was the Big Blizzard of eighty-six, eighty-seven. Froze damn near everyone here. Knew some of the ol'-timers that survived it, and they said if you walked across the state of Kansas into Colorado you would step on one dead animal after another. Ol' Flynn—this ol'-timer that's been dead for years—he had eighteen thousand head of cattle. Lost 'em all. Lost two cowboys too. Froze to death sittin' in the saddle up on Sand Creek Pass.

"Alex Swan had the T-Bar outfit then. He was mixed up with Tom Horn in the Swan Land and Cattle Company deal."

I asked what he remembered about Tom

Horn, one of the most controversial, mysterious and fascinating characters in Western history.

"Well, he was hung before I was born. I was born in 1906 and they hung him in 1903."

"He was hung in Laramie, wasn't he?"

"No, Cheyenne."

"Was he framed?" I asked. A lot of people thought he had been framed, that he really hadn't killed Willie Nichols.

Willie Nichols (left) was murdered at the age of fourteen. Tom Horn (right), accused and convicted of the murder, was hanged on the morning of November 20, 1903 in Cheyenne, Wyoming.

I was aware of the Tom Horn controversy because I had been planning a film on his life and research had been difficult since the accounts were conflicting and sketchy. He had at intervals in his life been a tracker and scout for the United States Army in its crusade to corral the Apache Indians (he was supposedly responsible for the capture of Geronimo), a stock company detective, a Pinkerton man, a United States marshal and a cowboy. Horn had lived with and spoke the language of the Apaches, learned braiding, roping and other skills from them and was the first rodeo cowboy before it was an organized sport. He was indisputably unique, a ruthless killer with no apparent morality, a man for hire. His amorality has been attributed to disillusionment with the United States government, after seeing first hand as an army scout the double standard on human rights it adopted in its dealings with the Indians. He is generally credited with single-handedly cleaning out the rustlers from Brown's Park, Utah, having managed the strange and somewhat mystical feat of scaring his victims by suggesting he was more than one man. He is a character who pops up frequently in the annals of Western history, though he is sparingly described. It is said he was innocent when he was hanged in Cheyenne in 1903 for the shooting death of a fourteen-year-old boy named Willie Nichols, that because of what he knew he had become a threat to the cattlemen who had hired him to rid the area of rustlers and so he was framed by Jo Lefors.

"Do you think he killed the boy?" I asked Roupe.

"Damn right. He admitted it, didn't he?"

I reminded him that a lot of people felt his confession had been tricked out of him while he was drunk.

"Naw, he was a braggart when he got to drinkin.' He cut up that kid with that knife and ol' Hailey sent him down to Brown's Park and that's where he killed ol' Matt Rash."

Matt Rash was a nephew of Davy Crockett. He was also a noted rustler much wanted by the cattlemen. In 1900 Horn ambushed him

Caught in a moment of fellowship: (left to right) Matt Rash, Mike Nicholson, and Bill Harris. Rash was a nephew of Davy Crockett.

as he stepped out of his cabin in Brown's Park.

"Then he killed that one-armed Owens out of Laramie, who was a woman, the one the big cowmen tried to run off her homestead. The cowmen didn't want to see these homesteaders in there. That's what started the Johnson County War. People out of Buffalo cornered them people out of Kaycee on the Teasdale Ranch, got a load of

$18,000.00
REWARD

Union Pacific Railroad and Pacific Express Companies jointly, will pay $2,000.00 per head, dead or alive, for the six robbers who held up Union Pacific mail and express train ten miles west of Rock Creek Station, Albany County, Wyoming, on the morning of June 2nd, 1899.

The United States Government has also offered a reward of $1,000.00 per head, making in all $3,000.00 for each of these robbers.

Three of the gang described below, are now being pursued in northern Wyoming; the other three are not yet located, but doubtless soon will be.

DESCRIPTION: One man about 32 years of age; height, five feet, nine inches; weight 185 pounds; complexion and hair, light; eyes, light blue; peculiar nose, flattened at bridge and heavy at point; round, full, red face; bald forehead; walks slightly stooping; when last seen wore No. 8 cow-boy boots.

Two men, look like brothers, complexion, hair and eyes, very dark; larger one, age about 30; height, five feet, five inches; weight, 145 pounds; may have slight growth of whiskers; smaller one, age about 28; height, five feet, seven inches; weight 135 pounds; sometimes wears moustache.

Any information concerning these bandits should be promptly forwarded to Union Pacific Railroad Company and to the United States Marshal of Wyoming, at Cheyenne.

UNION PACIFIC RAILROAD COMPANY.
PACIFIC EXPRESS COMPANY.

Omaha, Nebraska, June 10th, 1899.

straw, put it on a wagon, set it on fire and run it up against ol' Nate Champion's cabin. That's how they run him out of there and killed him. Then they started killin' some horses and the army came in and stopped it."

"Were there many people killed in the war?"

"Naw, truth is there wasn't."

I offered Garvin Taylor's opinion that the Johnson County War had been much exaggerated.

"That's right. There was Nate and this fella that was in the cabin with him who went out to get water. They got him. See, Nate was with the homesteaders and the big cowmen claimed they was rustlin', but they wasn't doin' nothin', jes' tryin' to run some cattle and stay alive. Hell, I run cattle in this country when the land was free, the grass was free. But them big cowmen wanted to take everything and keep it for themselves. They had some trouble with the sheepmen but they finally worked it out and settled down and lived like people should. But these people today, they don't have no respect for anything no more. Take the big corporations, big companies, or even the people in the towns like Lander. You can walk down the street, they look at ya like they was mad at ya about somethin'—greedy and jealous."

I asked him why that was.

"Oh, jes' greedy. Want everything for themselves. It's a fact, lad, you'll see as you go. Take the ranch people. They used to work together, help each other. But that's gone—you don't have neighbors anymore!"

I asked how he felt about the big corporations and companies coming into the area.

"You've always got them kind of people. Wyoming is loaded with coal—they can strip-mine it, put it back to seed, and it ain't gonna hurt nothin'."

I asked if he was sure that it would happen. Or was it just a promise? Was it really possible?

He gave me a cold squint. "Ya know, any time you get someone tryin' to do good for the people you're gonna get someone right away set up against it. Always. Let 'em go ahead and mine this. It'd put a lot of people to work. And that's what people need—work!"

He began to tap the table emphatically with his forefinger.

"So they can make a livin'! Ya know somethin', lad, I've seen two world wars and I see this crap we keep fightin' over in Korea and Vietnam and all. All right, let me tell you somethin'."

The rhythmic tapping built in intensity.

"You take these people here, and as long as you keep them workin' so they can buy beefsteaks and potatoes and eat like people should, you can get along with 'em. But take that biscuit away from 'em and then that's somethin' else buddy! They're gonna get madder'n hell."

Now he was pounding the table.

"Like this Rockyfeller. Now, why in hell does he want the government to bail New York out? He was governor, why didn't he keep 'em bailed out? Now he wants the taxpayers—you and me—to bail 'em out. Now you take old John D. Years ago, when he tried to take all this out here in Wyoming, I was here. He wanted to throw what he didn't take for himself into a park up there in Jackson and cut the cowmen off from their summer range. Them cowmen were 'bout ready to hang him. Why do you think this

Three Wyoming outlaws: (left to right) Dudley Champion, Martin Allison Tisdale, and Nathan Champion. It was the killing of Nate Champion that initiated the Johnson County War.

"What kind of kooks?"

"The kind who would murder someone for kicks or no good reason."

I asked if it was much different from the old days. He evaded the question.

"You take a lot of those goofs like the two boys that killed that social worker down at Devil's Slide. They cut him up with a knife—no reason. Never had a chance, that fella. I used to guard at the Wyoming State Penitentiary and I'd check the records of those in for murder and always the people they murdered didn't have a chance in the world. I learned one thing on the range. I had a lot of them kind threaten to kill me when they got out of jail, and I'd tell 'em, 'You name the time and the place and I'll damn sure be there.' I never heard from the bastards."

Nelson fella wants to be vice-president and all that crap? All that man wants is power. Him and his brother David. Why, with all his money, is he comin' out here and buyin' one of these ranches, payin' a million dollars for it? He's jes' gettin' himself one big headache the way ranchin' is goin'."

"Do you think ranching is going out?"

"It's *been* out for a long time. *Real* ranchin' went out in Tom Horn's time." He let out a long slow breath and became silent.

"What do you do now, Larry?"

"Oh, nothin'. Mosey around Lander sometimes. Don't much care for it there. People, new people comin' in, look at me funny. Lot of kooks around these days. Don't know what's got into people."

At this point Donna came into the bar. I never did find out her last name, she was just Donna to the folks there at the Mercantile. There was a vague reference to her having come up from Denver after a divorce. Like so many, she was looking to dodge the mantle of accountability and searching for a clean slate. She had a powerful persona, an ability to search the immediate atmosphere, size it up and bring it to her. She had a radiant if slightly raw countenance, warm and well-traveled, pain and pleasure

Below: The author inspects a homemade
wind generator system and (right) talks
with its engineer, John Mionczynski, on
the front steps of the cabin he built with
materials no one else wanted.

brought to an attractive boil in her eyes. She
quickly commanded center stage by rolling a
leg over a bar stool while ordering a beer.

After giving us all a friendly but wary
scan, she started up a conversation with Dan
and Arlinka. Arlinka is easy to meet and
interested in everyone and everything, and
Dan, having been a salesman, fears no social

beast. Donna explained she had been out alone trying to get an antelope, with no luck. She looked haggard, as if she had been over the Wind River Range by foot.

Within minutes everyone had decided to go see the house John Mionczynski had built himself. I was for that. I said good-bye to Larry Roupe and thanked him for a rewarding conversation.

"Sure, lad. Any time."

We walked the mile or so to John's place. It is a small, economically shaped log cabin nestled in the thick of a pine forest. A short distance from the cabin is a crude windtower, a wind generator sitting atop an oil-rig-shaped stack. A wire leads down the top to a closed box at the bottom that houses a 12-volt battery. The cabin itself was wonderful—quaint and serviceable— everything designed and built for need. As a result, it had all the warmth and flavor people pay architects and designers thousands of dollars to effect. There was evidence of John's ingenuity everywhere. It made me more aware than ever how far we have strayed from design that reflects real as opposed to manufactured need.

John's friends had helped him build the house and people from the town had pitched in too. He has a home built out of man's waste material: barnwood from a torn-down cabin, pine and aspen logs from a highway construction job, abandoned machine parts, discarded tools, recycled materials, old rubber, scraps, pieces. He is nested on ten acres in the midst of a pine forest where no one can touch him. He has a cut stack of dead fall wood for the winter, as well as goats roaming nearby for milk.

We went into the cabin, took a potato from the root cellar, opened a beer and talked.

"I worry about this becoming radical chic," John said, "with people coming in from Rock Springs, where the big plant is, and California. I love it here, but if the flow gets too great, I'll pick up and haul."

Someone else showed up: a young,

attractive, green-eyed woman from Kentucky.

"What are you doing here?" I asked.

"Living," she answered.

It was said straight and simply, not with the spaced-out smugness of the drugged counterculture types of the sixties who challenged, "I dare you to dig my world." She meant it. And in that word was the essence of what I had experienced in Atlantic City: good people from all over, Kentucky, Denver, Iowa, New York, working together, yet maintaining a certain independence. There is a return-to-the-land movement, and it is alive and well in Atlantic City.

I chatted for a while with Green-eyes and John, feeling the warmth of the stove, watching shadows grow larger. Terry Minger and Arlinka Blair were bloating themselves on Ritz crackers and cheese. Terry was clearly impressed by the resourcefulness he saw here.

He graduated from the University of Kansas and moved to Boulder, Colorado, a challenging place with room to move around in. Terry has a restless mind and a probing spirit. In addition, he has a pragmatic underpinning that, to my mind, makes him a good candidate for any future planning trust. Not held by past notions or credos, he is willing to listen, look and learn. Another key quality, and great plus on this trip, was his fine, easy humor that allowed him to go with whatever came along; a sense of adventure that, as it turned out, we would all need.

Finally it was time to move on. Arlinka was promising quilted work from her Turkish yarn and expressing the hope that they might all meet again. We said good-bye, and as we walked up the hill to find a place to camp for the night, I thought—Larry Roupe is wrong. He has neighbors right here.

Cattle Kate.

SOUTH PASS CITY

The next day we moved out along the trail over to South Pass City, a famous boom town during the days of the westward railroad expansion. South Pass's history has never been completely told. Because of its strategic location—it's a twenty-mile-wide niche in the barrier mountains of the Continental Divide—South Pass became immensely important in the move west. Such famous Western outlaws as Jim Bridger, Dr. Marcus Whitman, Kit Carson, Jedediah Smith, Broken Hand Fitzpatrick, Butch Cassidy, Jesse Ewing, Isom Dart and Tom Horn passed through here. Thousands of emigrants came through in wagon trains between 1841 and 1869, the latter being the year the Transcontinental Railroad was completed. Just through the pass the routes divided—one coursing south to Fort Bridger and the Salt Lake Valley, and the other branching northwestward to the Oregon Territory. In 1842 gold was discovered in the region, and by 1863 prospecting was the chief industry, although the area was still plagued by Indian attacks. In the fall of 1865 South Pass was officially laid out as a townsite. In 1868 miners began flocking in from California, Nevada and elsewhere. Overnight the population swelled from a few

South Pass City, 1875. Thousands of emigrants in wagon trains passed through this historic town between the years 1841–1869. Just beyond the pass the routes divided—one coursing south to Fort Bridger and the Salt Lake Valley and the other branching northwestward to the Oregon Territory.

Jedediah Strong Smith, a renowned woodsman, led many parties into the previously unexplored areas of Wyoming, Idaho, Utah, and Colorado.

hundred to more than five thousand.

The jail, as one can see today, could have been designed for Devil's Island. Among its many residents were Jesse Ewing, a hard-case outlaw who had been clawed so badly by a grizzly bear he was nicknamed "The Ugliest Man in South Pass," and Isom Dart, a black ex-gandy dancer who became a rustler and then a hired horse trainer for outlaws. He and Ewing were put in the same cell because of the overflow clientele, and Ewing didn't take to rooming with a black. He forced Dart to kneel so he could use his back as a table. Dart consented because he feared being hanged by the miners if he retaliated for his abuse. The score was settled later, however, when a friend of Dart's blew Ewing's head off. Dart went to Brown's Park where he raised and trained horses for the Wild Bunch and rustled cattle until his death at the hands of Tom Horn in 1900.

Here in South Pass, John Browning,

inventor of the Browning automatic rifle, had his first gun shop and Buffalo Bill worked for the Pony Express. Calamity Jane lived in the town during the period that gave rise to her reputation.

By 1890 the mines, which had produced millions, were played out and the town was given over to the outlaw element and gamblers. In 1896 it became a link in the chain of hideouts established by Butch Cassidy and the Wild Bunch.

Today South Pass City is another tintype out of yesteryear. Maybe it was the time of year. Maybe the time of day. Maybe the cold temperature. But I felt I was standing where man had not set foot for nearly a century. It was as barren as a Salvador Dali landscape except for a wooden boardwalk. How could it be that so much history had happened in this warped miniature town? Everything seemed so small, as in dollhouses. Were rooms really that small and beds that narrow and stairs that cramped?

No one was there when we first arrived. We walked silently around peering in windows—the saloon, the post office, the general store, the hotel with its honeymoon suite, the jail, the dugout. Echoes of past romances, of wild and lawless times, of drunken brawls. How did they keep order in this place? Was it just too cold? No, people have needs no matter where they are.

Soon Gary and Carla Stevenson, a young, pleasant couple who are the custodians of South Pass, came by and opened all the old buildings for us. We stood at the bar and I could hear the faint calliope of voices and music and chips and glass breaking—a brawling innocence, a purity of good times.

And now a cameo for your locket: the general store with its soaps and oils and cure-alls, the tobacco and spirits. Even then it paid to advertise—Bloomer girls illustrating soaps and cigars, moustached men with waved hair parted in the middle, arms folded to look bold and sure, advocating shaving cream. Train company ads promoting this new and exciting way to travel.

Then the hotel hallways, barely wide enough to walk through. Upstairs were several bedrooms that seemed to be on top of each other and, at the end of the hall, the bridal suite. The poor honeymooners, I thought. What was to keep some wild-eyed, boozed-up Jack who'd been mining or in the mountains for three months from roaring through the marital screen and spoiling the fun, or downright stealing it? Privacy had

different boundaries in the West.

And the jail: small and claustrophobic, it was built to drive sane men mad. As we stood in the pressed, dark confines of the individual cells that no man could withstand unless he were in a drunken stupor or unconscious, I couldn't conceive of spending five minutes in such fetid confinement without going berserk.

Gary told us about Esther Morris, one of the founders of the Women's Suffrage movement. It was here in South Pass City that her idea was born and gained momentum. He pointed to a hillside dugout that resembled a lateral mine shaft or a root cellar—just an old wooded barricade door in

Marcus Whitman, a missionary, was instrumental in securing the Oregon Territory for the United States. Born in Rushville, New York in 1802, he died during an Indian attack in Oregon in 1847.

the side of the hill. Here women and children would seek shelter during Indian raids or fights with outlaws, or get out of the way of opposing interests in the train construction. During one hiding, Esther Morris sold her idea to a Mrs. Wright, the wife of a district judge, who put the arm on her husband, who in turn promoted its passage into legislation. Esther Morris and the Suffrage movement were on their way. Sometime later Esther herself became a judge in South Pass.

Having one of the wildest reputations in the West, South Pass was truly an open city,

Perhaps no other lawman was as effective in tracking down outlaws as Charles Siringo. Leaving behind a career as a Texas cowboy, he became a feared Pinkerton operative, successfully infiltrated the Wild Bunch, and captured some of its members.

raw and chaotic, with a steady influx of transients, miners, gold diggers, thieves, outlaws, Pinkertons, whores, gamblers, hustlers, cattlemen, railroad construction workers—and a few stalwart merchants who ran the town mercantile. One wonders if *they* weren't a bit crazy too.

As I stood in the center of the main street looking away to the gray-brown hills beyond, I was lost in the memory of the rich, raucous innocence of the frontier: its rails and boardwalks and tents and snake-oil eagerness, its indomitable spirit. All was quiet now, faded into a still freeze in the later afternoon, a sepia time. It was a flashback to the early promise of our national fiber, an echo now. I wondered if that rich and vibrant part of our heritage wasn't an echo as well.

South Pass City was for me, finally, a sad place but it did offer us one present-day quality to cheer. It was the first stop on our way where we sensed a major attempt to preserve a part of our national heritage.

I t was time to travel by four-wheel vehicle to our next horse-and-saddle station— Brown's Park, Utah. This was a drive of about 125 miles, from South Pass to the Park via Rock Springs, Wyoming.

Dan and Arlinka and Jonathan drove in our "Outlaw Trail Jeep," while Terry Minger and I rode in a rented car we soon nicknamed

$12,000 REWARD.

Office of United States Marshal,
Cheyenne, Wyoming,
June 3, 1899.

To Whom It May Concern:

On Friday morning, June 2, 1899, a party of masked men, supposed to be six in number, took possession of the United States Mail, near Wilcox station, Albany county, Wyoming, in Union Pacific cars Numbers 1120 and 1190, by the use of dynamite and dangerous weapons. Warrants have been issued for their arrest under the provisions of Section 5472, Revised Statutes of the United States. Under Circular No. 532 of the Postmaster General of the United States a reward of ONE THOUSAND DOLLARS is offered for the arrest and conviction of each person violating the provisions of the said Section 5472 of the Revised Statutes of the United States.

By circular issued this date the UNION PACIFIC RAILWAY COMPANY offers the sum of ONE THOUSAND DOLLARS for the capture, dead or alive of each and every person proven to be the persons or either of them who held up the first section of train Number one, as above described, on the morning of June 2, 1899.

The following is a partial description of the robbers: Leader of party about fifty years old; five feet seven or eight inches tall; thin, round nose; large eyes with small eyeballs; wore slouch hat, light canvas coat; weight, about 160 pounds.

Second man: dark complexion; black, woolly hair; wore slouch hat, dark suit; about five feet nine or ten inches tall; weight, about 170 pounds.

Third man: about five feet, eight or nine inches tall; black suit; dark hair; weight about 160 to 170 pounds.

Fourth man: about five feet six inches tall; dark complexion; wore gray hat. pants inside boots; weight about 160 pounds.

Fifth man: about five feet six inches tall; weight about 145 pounds; wore cowboy white hat with drooping brim, black leather shoes; canvas leggings, brown overalls or corduroy pants, light, medium length overcoat; spoke with Texan twang; carried carbine with long wood on barrel reaching to within five inches of end.

Sixth man: about five feet eight inches tall; weight about 150 pounds; stubby, sandy beard.

The robbers secured several thousand dollars in National Bank currency, in bills of the denomination of twenty and one hundred dollars, of the First National Bank of Portland Oregon, series 1553. and valueless because not signed by the officers of that bank.

Please communicate with any Sheriff, Deputy Marshal or other peace officer, or with me at Cheyenne, Wyoming. should you have or obtain any information of the above described persons.

FRANK A. HADSELL. U. S. Marshal.
District of Wyoming.

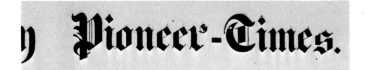

Pioneer-Times.

HILLS). TUESDAY MORNING, NOVMEBER 2. 1897.

BANK ROBBERS BREAK JAIL.

Inveigle Jailer Mansfield into a Trap---Slug and Lock Him in and Skip.

Robbers of Belle Fourche Bank and Murderdr Moore Take French Leave.

At 8:45 o'clock Sunday evening Thomas O'Day, Walter Puntney, and Thomas and Frank Roberts, alias Jones, a part of the famous Hole-in-the Wall gang of outlaws who robbed the Belle Fourche bank last June, and William Moore, colored, who shot and killed Henry Staley, near Englewood, about two months ago, and was confined in jail awaiting action of the grand jury, escaped from the Lawrence county jail at this place. They accomplished their design and gained their liberty by a cleverly planned and well executed piece of work, by catching Jailer John Mansfield off his guard.

Though early in the evening and just as the church goers were returning home from evening services, many of them passing the jail at the time, the five desperadoes broke for liberty and in the darkness disappeared as though they had evaporated. The delivery was discovered almost instantly by Sheriff Plunkett, who resides directly opposite the jail on Sherman street and though he started in pursuit at once, he could not obtain even the least

cher found a handkerchief on McGovern hill above the Congregational church, and carefully marked the spot where it was found. The handkerchief was identified as one that O'Day had secured from an Indian prisoner in a trade. The sheriff telegraphed to Lincoln, Neb., after several blood-hounds and it is believed by taking them to the spot where the handkerchief was found and giving them the scent the hounds will track the men to their hiding places.

All sorts of rumors were afloat all day, and the excitement ran high Crowds of men surged around the court house and jail, eager for some news. The sheriff believed the robbers had taken a route along McGovern hill and were headed toward the southwest. His theory was confirmed when he was informed that on Saturday five saddle horses were led to a place near Maurice station, on the B. & M. railroad in Spearfish canyon and were being held there, saddled, evidently awaiting the appearance of riders. Later Sheriff Plunkett heard that four men passed Whit's half way ranch on the Carbonate road at 11 o'clock Sunday night. Putting these together it was plausible enough that the fugitives were making for the horses by the way of the Carbonate road and Squaw Creek. There were strong suspicions that the plot to accomplish the escape was made by friends on the outside.

Later it was learned that four men were seen on the False Bottom road at or near Garden City and posses were started out on both trails. Sheriff Plunkett offered a reward of $250 for the capture of the five men, or $50 for each. Circulars were printed and sent out in every direction, while every sheriff in Wyoming and Montana and the Black Hills counties was notified to

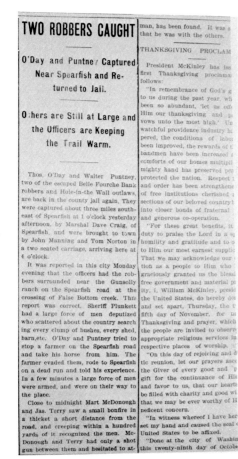

TWO ROBBERS CAUGHT

O'Day and Puntney Captured Near Spearfish and Returned to Jail.

Others are Still at Large and the Officers are Keeping the Trail Warm.

Thos. O'Day and Walter Puntney, two of the escaped Belle Fourche Bank robbers and Hole-in-the Wall outlaws, are back in the county jail again. They were captured about three miles southeast of Spearfish at 1 o'clock yesterday afternoon, by Marshal Dave Craig, of Spearfish, and were brought to town by John Manning and Tom Norton in a two seated carriage, arriving here at 4 o'clock.

It was reported in this city Monday evening that the officers had the robbers surrounded near the Gunsolly ranch on the Spearfish road at the crossing of False Bottom creek. This report was correct. Sheriff Plunkett had a large force of men deputized who scattered about the country searching every clump of bushes, every shed, barn, etc. O'Day and Puntney tried to stop a farmer on the Spearfish road and take his horse from him. The farmer evaded them, rode to Spearfish on a dead run and told his experience. In a few minutes a large force of men were armed, and were on their way to the place.

Close to midnight Mart McDonough and Jas. Terry saw a small bonfire in a thicket a short distance from the road, and creeping within a hundred yards of it recognized the men. McDonough and Terry had only a shot gun between them and hesitated to at-

man, has been found. It was a that he was with the others.

THANKSGIVING PROCLAM

President McKinley has iss first Thanksgiving proclama follows:

"In remembrance of God's g to us during the past year, wh been so abundant, 'let us off Him our thanksgiving and p vows unto the most high.' Un watchful providence industry h pered, the conditions of labo been improved, the rewards of t bandmen have been increased a comforts of our homes multipli mighty hand has preserved pe protected the nation. Respect a and order has been strengthene of free institutions cherished sections of our beloved country into closer bonds of fraternal and generous co-operation.

"For these great benefits, it duty to praise the Lord in a s humility and gratitude and to o to Him our most earnest supplic That we may acknowledge our tion as a people to Him who graciously granted us the blessi free government and material p ity, I, William McKinley, presid the United States, do hereby de and set apart, Thursday, the t fifth day of November, for n Thanksgiving and prayer, which the people are invited to observ appropriate religious services in respective places of worship.

"On this day of rejoicing and d tic reunion, let our prayers asce the Giver of every good and gift for the continuance of His and favor to us, that our hearts be filled with charity and good wi that we may be ever worthy of H neficent concern.

"In witness whereof I have her set my hand and caused the seal United States to be affixed.

"Done at the city of Washin this twenty-ninth day of Octobe

These newspaper articles from Deadwood, South Dakota tell of the Belle Fourche Bank robbery in 1897.

"The Red Lemon." The incongruity of traveling along this country in a carriage made up in assembly-line haste was unsettling. (This discordant note turned into a humorous one when we attempted to transform the Red Lemon into a horse-drawn wagon. The Mormons would have marveled at many of the places through which we nursed that horse-drawn car.) Riding along at future-shock speeds, we were caught in the loveliness of the wide vistas on the Continental Divide and the bountiful herds of antelope, buck and deer. They were so abundant and so bold that in many instances they grouped in great clumps alongside the road.

The ride to Rock Springs is flat and wide. The range country spills into an alluvial fan from the high passes at the Continental Divide. October here is a gray-streaked sky. The summer colors that have not yet faded stand out in contrast. It is a lovely time, the time just before winter. There seems to be a stillness in the air, the calm before the storm.

This reward poster was issued in Cheyenne, Wyoming by United States Marshal Frank Hadsell, who was later killed by Kid Curry.

The great herds roam in freedom as though under some special dispensation before their execution. For tomorrow the hunt will begin and these pastoral stretches of quiet beauty will become a battleground. Military-like advances will be made on a defenseless, retreating species. Such are the wages of progress and pleasure. Some join this onslaught to satisfy a genuine need.

Two men of Silver City, New Mexico.

Many farmers, ranchers and sheepmen hunt to provide for their families. Hunting was once part of the natural balance of things. But now, these genuine hunters are lost in a vast army, many from out of state, invading for the sheer pleasure of the sport. Many will pull into diners, gas stations, or neighborhoods with their grills, pickup beds or rear seats draped with the carcasses of their victims. These are the ones we feared as we made our way south—the day-glo-hatted hunters who are trigger-happy their first day out. To be in the vicinity is to expose yourself to stray bullets or poor shots or scavengers with poor eyesight, or sometimes drunken ones. We beat a hasty retreat to that part of the Outlaw Trail that is sufficiently distant from any given road to test even the hardiest of scavengers.

Today Rock Springs speaks for itself. One has only to see it—a power-plant boom town stretching out in the middle of a vast plain with transmission lines, trailers, rubble-strewn roads and the back sides of signs, signs telling you what will happen here, what to buy and where to buy it. A complete portrait of a transitory existence. I was immediately struck by the harsh contrast with South Pass City. Did Rock Springs once look like South Pass City? Perhaps in another century someone will

come upon Rock Springs and wonder why we were so oblivious of our surroundings and our aesthetic needs.

The history of Rock Springs is colorful but, ironically, the same migrant vision that established it is now threatening its stability and we are unable to stop this destruction with common sense. The power plant has replaced the gold rush drawing hundreds, thousands, of transitory workers—four-year tenants with portable lives. The power plant brings with it boom-town inflation, water and sewage services, schools and recreation facilities. It may leave behind closed rotting storefronts, untended timber, broken glass and bewildered taxpayers to pick up the

Rock Springs, Wyoming
at the turn of the century.

pieces and deal with the psychological depression that often follows in the wake of all this.

It was here that I had my first real flash of ambivalence. I was bothered by what I saw, yet I have a genuine love for the people I met along the way and wondered if we don't too often impose an aesthetic vision on those who choose to gamble on the risks a developing trend may bring. One cannot in any way know unless one has lived it, the depression of continued unemployment; one cannot feel what it is like to stand in soil turned to dust, unable to provide for self and family, and think only of the beauties of nature and the merits of a colorful heritage. To stand atop an apparent wasteland with no recourse or hope and know that a few feet below is a resource so rich that people and money will flock to its uncovering is a very real dilemma. The fiber of these people can only be admired. It is for the most part a quality of grit and courage that is ancestral. And in a system where change is inevitable, one can only hope that change can be made without trading off too much on the qualities of the land and the people, gained through years of pioneering, hardship and enterprise. I realized this as we rode southward to Brown's Park and I was silenced in hard thought.

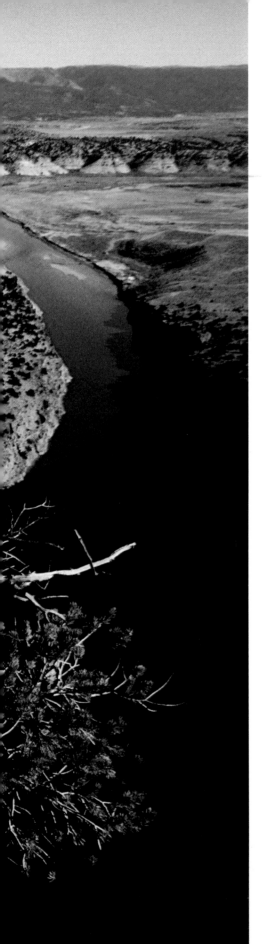

BROWN'S PARK

No single location in the West, and certainly none on the Outlaw Trail, has had such a varied history as Brown's Park. Located at the northeast border of Utah and Colorado just over the Wyoming line to the south, Brown's Park is a forty-mile square, half in Utah and half in Colorado. Surrounded by Diamond Mountain, Douglas Mountain and the Owi-ya-kuts Plateau, it is cut through the middle by the famed Green River, now a popular raft-floating mecca for sportsmen.

The earliest-known reference to Brown's Park was made in 1650 in the writings of Father Ortiz, a Spanish missionary. The Spanish had constructed a series of forts in this region but the Indians set fire to most of them, driving the Spanish away. In 1825 the expedition of William H. Ashley and his fur trappers penetrated the valley in bull-boats along the Green River. In 1827 Kit Carson traded here among the Ute and Shoshone Indians. The same year a trader named Baptiste Chalifoux came to the valley with his Indian wife and the valley was named in his honor under his alias "Baptiste Brown." From then on, Brown's Park was the most popular trading center in the region and became the home of many

The Green River passes through Brown's Park at the Wyoming-Utah-Colorado border. Here many outlaws and ranchers enjoyed a peaceful co-existence.

Jim Baker, an early guide, pioneer, fur trapper, and settler.

trappers whose names are now synonymous with the history of fur trading in the Far West: Jim Bridger, Kit Carson, Jim Baker, Jack Robinson and many others.

In 1849 the Cherokee Indians, recently uprooted from their homelands in Georgia, drove a herd of cattle through Brown's Park on their way to California. Thereafter, Brown's Park became a favorite wintering place for cattle herds being driven from Texas to Montana. Traces of the famed Cherokee Trail can still be seen today.

Outlaws knew of the advantages afforded by the Park's isolation as early as 1850, when they began to plague the wagon trains streaming westward along the Oregon-Mormon Trail. Traveling in loose-knit gangs, they raided the horses and cattle of the wagon trains and wintered the stolen herds in Brown's Park until the herds could be safely driven out and disposed of.

The largest influx of outlaws came during and shortly after the Civil War, when deserters and the ragtag element of the war drifted into the Park for refuge. Before long these nomadic groups were organized into the Tip Gault Gang, the Tom Crowley Gang, the "Mexican Joe" Herrera Gang, the "Doc" Bender Gang, the Diamond Mountain Gang, the McCarty Gang, the Brush Creek Gang, the Rock Springs Gang and many others.

There were legitimate ranchers and settlers in Brown's Park, too, such as John Jarvie, a Scotsman, who owned and operated the only permanent store and saloon, and Charley Crouse, the Hoy Brothers and the Bassett family. In order to survive among the outlaws, the ranchers had to appease them. The outlaws, in turn, were content to let the ranchers pretty much alone since they were valuable friends in time of trouble. Butch Cassidy cultivated rancher friendships to great advantage.

he law didn't come to Brown's Park until the turn of the century. It is said that the Park was the most lawless place in the entire West. The only law was that of the fastest

gun. (Some 170 graves are known throughout the Park.) But even without the standard form of civilized law and order there was a systematic, if rough, social order. There was a school for children of the Park, the Jarvies' store, a blacksmith shop, saloon and other accoutrements of community living. Conspicuously absent of course was a jail.

Most of the gravesites, markers, cabins, saloons and hideouts are gone now, buried by time, development and lack of interest. There are only a few ranches left in the Utah section and the Allen Ranch is the main one. Marie Allen is the granddaughter of one of the first settlers in the valley. Her father was a homesteader who took over the cabin that once belonged to Butch Cassidy and had been used many times by outlaws retreating through the Park.

I had been forewarned that getting to the Park wasn't exactly a navigator's delight, especially at night. For fifty miles there is a paved road and then dirt and a long winding descent into darkness. The road resists vehicular traffic and before long the Red Lemon was groaning at the turns. Twigs, rocks, dust all brushed past us as though we were ramming a blockade. We were trying to find the Allen Ranch.

The ranch is on the northern edge of the Park. There are no lights to guide you there, no road signs and, in some cases, no real road. Possessed by the notion that we would be pulled along by divine guidance, we plowed a furrow through the dusty night and got totally lost. Occasionally we passed a hunter sitting in his camper-home, all warm and comfortable, portable TV on, drink in hand, waiting. We passed out of Wyoming and into Utah.

The moon came up but its light made no difference. The road was now desolate except for an occasional clover leaf. We no longer knew whether we were heading south or north—or where. We had been told by one of the friendly hunters we passed to follow the road to the first left and then go down a long canyon. A typical cowboy direction: "Head out to that juniper, turn left, go west to the Rocky Mountains and

may the Good Lord bless your skies."

We took the first left and went up on a mountain. "This is the highest canyon I've ever been in," Terry said in droll comment. Finally a marker saying "Welcome to Wyoming" told us we were on the wrong track. We retraced, circled, stopped, went on. It was blind and desperate, and funny. The car was behaving like a ship breaking up on a reef and I wanted to abandon it. Terry reminded me how cold it would be if we did. Suddenly, like a small island that pops up out in the Caribbean, there it was, a single light—the Allen Ranch. We went in and met up with Ed Abbey and Kim Whitesides, two late joiners who had arrived separately and were already ensconced by a warm fire, having a good talk, and the rancher's

Uncle Jack Robinson (far right), whose cabin, built on the Henry fork of the Green River in 1835, was used by frontiersmen such as Jim Bridger, John C. Frémont, Kit Carson, John Wesley Powell, and John (Jeremiah) Johnson.

Overleaf: When the Green River was dammed to form the recreational area of Flaming Gorge, Utah, many cabins and homesteads sank beneath tons of water.

sound of a phonograph needle being pressed down on a record. His slow, economical, underwater-like movements conjure up memories of Haight-Ashbury. But he is a Mormon from Salt Lake, a successful artist who now lives in New York and thinks herb diets and Bob Dylan are his salvation. No amount of acquired sophistication can hide the child who loves the outdoors, adventure, exploring new areas and just going with the flow. Like Abbey, he is not what he appears to be.

The next day, after a welcome good night's sleep, we waited for Kerry Boren who had had to leave us in Lander and was to rejoin us here. Kerry was indispensable for this leg of the trip because he knew the history of the area so well. He was born in the nearby town of Green River, Wyoming, and raised in Manila, Utah, on the western edge of Brown's Park where the Flaming Gorge Reservoir now stands. His grandfather, he told us, knew Butch Cassidy and occasionally provided the Wild Bunch with food and fresh horses when they rode through the area to escape the law.

It was almost noon by the time Boren arrived and we straightened out our saddle packs and camp equipment. Our mounts were not in the best of shape. Unfortunately it was the time of year when cattle are

brought to slaughter and horses are worked to the breaking-point. We joked about how relieved we were not to be outlaws in the heat of chase because with these horses we would be goners. It was a comic getaway. I had a horse that thought sideways and Terry Minger had one with concrete shocks. Since he hadn't ridden much in his life and not at all in recent years, this horse was going to test his durability. Months sitting at a city desk and conducting seminars on urban planning had made Terry a mite tender for the ride, but his spirit was that of an experienced cowhand. Dan Arensmeier had the best horse, a fact that made me realize that Dan would probably be successful in his relocation and new job as a marketing consultant. He consistently ended up with the best horses. I never found out whether he made a deal the night before with the wrangler or whether he just had a knack for selecting stock, but he was always happy in the saddle. I tried to con him out of his choice this day because mine was so neurotic and independent, but, like any instinctual survivor, he politely declined. Boren's horse thought the trail was a circle and that charity began and ended at home. He couldn't get the horse to move out. Jonathan was too preoccupied with settings, focus and F-stop readings to care, and Arlinka didn't want to think about it. She just asked that whatever happened, she be kept safely in the middle. Kim and Ed took all this strife in stride, looking on with the

This famous portrait of the Wild Bunch was taken by John Schwartz in Fort Worth, Texas during the winter of 1900–1901. The men had gathered there after robbing a bank in Winnemucca, Nevada. Standing: Bill Carver, Harvey Logan. Sitting: Harry Longabaugh, Ben Kilpatrick, George LeRoy Parker.

amused air of seasoned riders who have seen it all before.

Bob Allen finally led us out onto the route and I asked Kerry Boren how his grandfather had known Butch Cassidy.

"My grandfather was Willard Scofield. The Parker and Scofield families had migrated to Utah together [Parker is Butch Cassidy's real name and these Parkers were his parents] in handcart companies in 1856." Boren then proceeded to rattle off a list of names and places and friends and relatives connected to one another by the pioneer bond. I had to stop him because this torrent was fogging my mind. I wanted to know about specific events involving the outlaws and the Wild Bunch. He told me his grandfather had been there when Butch Cassidy and the Sundance Kid put on a display of marksmanship at a place known as Connor Basin, not far from Manila where Kerry grew up.

"Butch would ride around a large tree, both hands on his rifle, placing bullet holes a neat inch apart all the way around the tree. The tree still stands, though it's nearly dead: all the bullet holes are still quite visible."

As we rode north from the ranch we crossed an old wooden bridge spanning the Green River. Bob Allen told us that next to it there was another bridge built by his

Esther Campbell lives in an old relic of a cabin that once belonged to John Jarvie, the first shopkeeper in Brown's Park. The Bassett cabin (opposite) is a landmark of outlaw history.

grandfather in 1900. "Just a crude bridge. It was used to transport sheep by tying pulleys to a cable and hanging a coal car from the pulleys so it would slide along." The remnants of the old cable and its moorings are still visible. "They would put a barge up against the bank, herd sheep into it, hook the cables to the barge, and the pulleys would move the barge across using the movement of the current, while a man in the back would steer. They'd transport sheep, horses, supplies, Indians, everything this way."

Kerry told us we had to meet Esther

Campbell, a seventy-eight-year-old woman who lives in an old relic of a cabin among the cottonwood trees on the other side of the bridge. The cabin once belonged to John Jarvie. He ran it as the first store in the Park, and then as a saloon, post office and blacksmith shop. He was murdered in the store in 1909. Esther and her late husband bought the cabin from Marie Allen's father, who had purchased it after Jarvie's murder. Esther has devoted much of her life to preserving this old site and many others.

She came outside to greet us, a spirited, untroubled woman, and led us around to "the Bassett Cabin" where Queen Ann and Josie Bassett, two famous outlaw sisters, once lived. Josie was Butch's girlfriend and entertained the Wild Bunch whenever they rode in.

Ann, known as "Queen Ann," was the older of the two, an attractive, lively woman who preferred "cowboyin' to bein' a lady" but was nevertheless lady enough to be the favorite among outlaws who ran in the area at the time. She and Josie had been raised and sent away to the finest schools by an indulgent father who wanted the best for his daughters, but they returned home in favor of a less disciplined and more adventuresome life.

Queen Ann was so named for her

Right: Herb and Josie Bassett in front of their cabin in Brown's Park, Utah.

Josie Bassett in 1953 at the ranch of John Jarvie.

well-educated manner, her impressive use of language, her penchant for entertaining outlaws, and her unique position as the only lady rustler. She was as fine a shot as any of the men around and could rope calves, drive cows and generally compete with the best outlaws at any sport of the time. Josie was as much a roisterer as her sister and together they made quite a pair. Queen Ann lived long and fully and died in 1958 in St. George, Utah. Josie stayed in the Park all her life and in later years became a real recluse and eccentric, refusing to sleep indoors,

Ann Bassett, known as Queen Ann, chose a life of cattle rustling over the refinements taught her at an Eastern boarding school.

much preferring to spend most of her time outside with the animals she kept around her cabin. Until her death a few years ago (she was in her nineties) she hunted and fished for most of her food and was viewed very much as a living monument to tougher, bygone days.

It was a wild and colorful time when the Park was the second main stronghold of the outlaws, Esther recalled. Now she is lonely, keeping whatever land is left and sparring with the Bureau of Land Management over rights and resisting offers to sell out. She

knows they would raze the old house but she can't hang on much longer.

She gave us each a crabapple from her tree and took us up on a hill behind the house to show us some graves, most of them unidentified. The few graves that were marked were done crudely. We saw the grave of Jesse Ewing, whose head was blown off at the neck by a blast from his own rifle in the hands of his partner, Duncan. Esther said the murder was supposed to have been the result of an argument over the attentions of a contortionist named Madame Forestall. (This information evoked a chorus of interest from our party.) Ironically, Ewing is buried next to one of his victims, a young man named Robinson whom Ewing is said to have disemboweled on the ice of the Green River in an argument over mining claims. Esther continued her morbid tour: "This one belonged to a man named Marshall, who was ambushed while crossing Red Creek in a wagon in 1887. When they found him, the birds had picked his eyes out."

Before we left, she told us to be sure to ride over to see old Doc Parsons' cabin which, through Marie Allen's diligent efforts, is the only cabin in that area that has been put on the Utah State Historical Register. We rode out through the cottonwoods that hugged Esther's cabin and onto a flat plain.

John Jarvie, a Scotsman, opened up a store in Brown's Park that became a central meeting place.

Obviously once a river bottom, it is now a wide boulder-strewn area with dense, low shrubbery of piñon and sagebrush. The horses' legs cracked through the dry brush in slow, even stride. The air was still and the view clear and distant. On the way Bob Allen talked of life in and around the park today and of people moving in from outside:

"It ain't that I don't like people. But it's hard sometimes to be with them. I feel funny. I've spent so long here on the range that I feel disconnected, sort of. Don't seem to have that much in common with a lot of folk. Can't understand why so many people are so sarcastic about so much. So many people seem sarcastic. Thought about goin' somewhere else, some other part of the world maybe, and try somethin' new. But cows and ranch work is all I know. Used to be I could herd them cows around all the time, never tired of it. Now I get mad when a cow won't move. Winters are so long and you set top of a horse waitin', watchin', freezin' your butt off, bones goin' still on you and business gettin' worse all the time, wonderin' all the while if it's worth it."

"Where did you go to school?" I asked.

"Over to Ladore School at the east end of the Park."

The school was built in 1911 by a lumberman out of Rock Springs. It was the only school for a hundred miles. Until it closed in 1947, it was the only school for ranchers' kids in the entire area. Though the old building is still sound, its future is dim.

Despite preservationists' efforts, it is slated for extinction because the Bureau of Land Management plans to make the area a wild game refuge.

At one point, Bob pulled up and stared around a thoughtful moment as though sniffing the wind for some clue.

"What are you doing?" I asked.

"Oh, jes' looking . . . was right about here where the old saloon was," he said, nodding up ahead. There was nothing but sage and rock. "Was here somewhere. . . . I remember when I was a kid we used to

Kim Whitesides and his horse taking a plunge after hitting a hole.

play in it, but I can't see it now. It's been weatherin' away for years. Can't remember when I saw it last, but it was pretty far gone then . . . can't find it now . . . guess it's rotted away. . . ."

We pulled into a shallow bank along the river and prepared to pitch camp for the night. It had been a long slow walk on horseback that day so a few of us decided to cut loose. We drove our horses across the river, using a sandbar as a bridge. Before long we were racing across it, yelling, slapping leather, herding imaginary cows. Suddenly Whitesides hit a hole and his horse disappeared from under him. We watched Kim sink gradually to his neck. Then, with a great burst of foam and splash, his horse lurched madly back up out of the water in an anxious effort to find sure footing. Kim was tossed like a kickball into the air and down into the water. With one hand still gripping the reins, he was dragged for thirty or forty feet until wisdom prevailed and he settled for chasing the horse through the waist-deep water pleading with him to return. This was all very comical until we thought of nightfall and the impending cold. We quickly made a fire to dry Whitesides out.

That night, over potatoes and beef and several cans of beer, we exchanged stories.

What is it about the warmth of a fire that so invites imaginative storytelling? We spoke of Tom Mix and other real-life cowboys who became movie stars, did their own stunts, and how they enjoyed that. We discussed Carlos Castaneda and the current search for a panacea in mysticism. Abbey squinted his disapproval and said he didn't hold much for it. He then talked of his time as a park ranger and what he had seen. Boren related more of the Park's history. It was like listening to a waterfall—names tumbling out of him like a hasty confession. I realized that for Kerry this experience was like a child being let loose in a candy store. He couldn't be sure of ever again capturing such an interested audience, so he relished the moment.

We were all fascinated by the parade of footloose, high-spirited, wild-riding outlaws who never knew permanence. In this place few lived to a ripe old age. So many were shot in the back by surprise or by accident, sometimes for no reason other than being drunk, bored, jealous, or just too happy. It was a place where no one asked

Butch Cassidy and Harry Tracy used this cabin near Ladore Canyon in Utah as one of their many hideouts.

many questions; a time when eyes in the back of the head was a necessary feature for survival. Life had a low premium and most everyone was prey to the whims of others. The Park had its own law and very little was sacred. It was a place where daughter murdered father and brother murdered brother. Shallow graves were common.

The fire simmered to a purple glow, the night chill came on, but that never daunted Kerry Boren's verbal onslaught. He was shining with enthusiasm as the rest of us, lulled by these stories blending into one another, began to succumb to much-needed sleep. The shadows of the Park's history came to life and we drifted off knowing that within a few miles' radius stood the old cabin of Matt Warner, one of the longest-surviving members of the Wild Bunch (he ended his life as a sheriff in Price, Utah); the crude rock-pile grave of Indian Joe, a drifter killed by Charley Crouse who had one of the first ranches at the mouth of the canyon; and the grave of "Mexican Joe" Herrera who was knifed in a card game and dragged to a hasty burial.

Morning. A thin white layer of frost was on everything. As people awakened, sleeping bags twisted spasmodically like slugs on a sidewalk after a rain. There were a few groans and then Whitesides began

Clockwise from lower left: *Arlinka Blair, Terry Minger, Robert Redford, Dan Arensmeier, and Kim Whitesides refresh themselves along the Green River.*

Left: *Silhouetted against the waters of the Green River, the author and Terry Minger share a quiet moment.*

Matt Warner, a brother-in-law of Tom McCarty and the son of a Mormon bishop, made several attempts to settle down. He bought a ranch in Brown's Park but soon, as he himself reported: "My cabin was crowded every night by a drinking, poker-playing, bragging crowd." After a twenty-year career as an outlaw, Warner was apprehended, tried, and sent to prison. Shortly thereafter he was pardoned by the governor and became the sheriff of Price, Utah.

making coffee with frozen hands. The morning fire crackled and bodies rustled. Everyone looked like hell with matted hair and slept-on faces, eyes red from the fire smoke of the night before. There were a lot of jokes about this being no place for a beauty contest, then breakfast, too much coffee, and we were off. Stiff with cold, we rode slowly toward Red Creek.

Along the way, the sun warming us, we traversed the cliffs that border the Green River about ten miles below the old Jarvie Ranch. It was tough going and one false move would have pitched horse and rider several hundred feet down to the river. Arlinka chose the high ground and walked partway. Ed Abbey became fascinated with rolling boulders off the edge and watching them explode like depth charges below.

I thought I had found a shortcut to a beached cove below the cliffs, but only succeeded in getting tangled up in a thicket of bulrushes and being tossed from my horse. I couldn't blame him, my navigation was hardly reassuring. I had to hike back up, leading the horse, to the accompaniment of guffaws from the others. Dan remarked that the horse probably had thrown me because he got a glimpse of my boots.

I had been getting a lot of heat on the subject of my boots since I bought them in Lander, Wyoming. I have always had a fondness for cowboy boots that are on the colorful side and I had bought a pair that were cream colored with a brown toe tip. The rest of the crew threatened to abandon the party if they had to ride with me wearing those boots. Jonathan Blair said he wanted to do a portrait of the boots (just the boots—he said I couldn't match their charisma); Arlinka coveted them for herself; Dan Arensmeier was afraid someone he knew might see him with me; and Kerry Boren bore up silently, looking like someone who had just discovered he had been saving counterfeit money.

After I had remounted we all separated and took different routes to a common point that overlooked Ladore Canyon to the south. This is a favorite launching spot for raft trips on the Green River. For about two hours we all rode solo. It was a good time, time to reflect and watch. A time to observe detail: the twist of a piñon root, the color and formation of the rich bedrock, the tracks of animals, an occasional flushing of a partridge as it took flight. And quiet.

Unbelievably, Jonathan Blair had covered most of this ground on foot. He personified the argument for energy gained through passion. His passion for the caught image was unquenchable. He seemed to be several people at once, a blur of motion and instruction: "Ride up there, get off the horse, turn him to the left, that's it—beautiful. Ed, ride in behind him, take your hat off—no,

you're covered by the piñon tree—move."

Ed, looking like a new army recruit at boot camp, fumbled vainly to obey these drill orders, then finally regained his self-esteem by telling Jonathan what he could do with his camera. Blair, not batting an eye, moved on, laughing. He put us to shame with his indomitable spirit, his unceasing good cheer and his physical endurance. He ran, walked, jumped, squatted, shouted, laughed, hooted, disappeared, then reappeared just moments later at an impossible distance away with a new set of instructions and requests. Then, finally, after an endless number of shutter snaps, fast reloads and a cacophony of mutterings, he appeared once again in our midst, as though he had never left, swinging effortlessly into our conversations and smiling his "grand to be alive" smile.

We came upon an area called Crouse Creek, named in honor of Charley Crouse, a friend and associate of the Wild Bunch who owned and operated a ranch in the area and frequently aided the outlaws. It was here that Tom Horn murdered Isom Dart in Dart's cabin. In this great grazing valley, surrounded by ridges with careful spotting-points on top, the outlaws had a natural fortress.

Crouse Creek is one of the most isolated spots in Brown's Park. Here one can find the remains of two fireplaces and cake ovens, constructed by Dr. John Parsons for the processing of copper ore. These ovens were favorite hideouts for hardcore outlaws, even

those rejected by the outlaw society of the Park itself.

After a long sweep through the canyon we wound south, back across the river, passing below the foot of Diamond Mountain and Cassidy Point. Kerry Boren told us that originally there was a cabin up on the Point, cleverly constructed beneath an overhanging ledge of rock and well out of sight, but commanding a view of the Park for

Charles and Mary Crouse were early settlers in Brown's Park. This photograph was taken shortly after they were married and set up house with a bunk bed, a buffalo robe, a dutch oven, and a frying pan.

Isom Dart: Slave, soldier, rodeo cowboy, cattle rustler, imposter. His life was ended by a single shot from Tom Horn's gun.

the Train Robbers Syndicate, but which later came to be known as the Wild Bunch. Over two hundred outlaws from all the prominent regional gangs were in attendance at that meeting, including members of the Hole-in-the-Wall gang, led by Flatnose George Curry together with Kid Curry and the Sundance Kid; the Powder Springs Gang, led by Dick "Doc" Bender; the Blue Mountain Gang; the Robbers Roost Gang; and the Diamond Mountain "Boys," among whom were Butch Cassidy, Elza Lay, Matt Warner and "Bub" Meeks.

"Even today," Kerry told us, "that meeting is remembered in Brown's Park as a wild celebration. During the day hardly an outlaw could be seen in the Park, but by early evening they came drifting in by twos and threes until the Crouse Ranch was an armed camp."

A conference of sorts was held in the cabin on Cassidy Point and it was agreed that an organization was needed, but there was a dispute between Cassidy and Kid Curry over who was best qualified to lead it. Tense moments passed until someone—probably Butch—came up with the idea of a contest.

It was a simple idea. They would meet again at Brown's Park in one year—on August 18, 1897. During that year two groups, one led by Cassidy, the other by Kid

miles in all directions. A trail led up to the Point from the Crouse Ranch below. Mrs. Crouse often cooked meals for the men hiding out up there, and her daughter Minnie (now Minnie Rasmussen) carried the food up to the men. Minnie, who is in her late nineties, was a girlfriend of Butch Cassidy.

It was at Cassidy Point in Brown's Park on August 18, 1896, that plans were formulated to organize what Cassidy proposed to call

Minnie Rasmussen, once Butch Cassidy's girlfriend, standing near the grave of Isom Dart in Brown's Park.

Curry, would pull off various robberies. Whoever was most successful, most spectacular and daring, would become the leader.

By the following August, Cassidy, with the aid of Elza Lay, "Bub" Meeks and Joe Walker, had successfully pulled off several robberies, the most spectacular being the robbery of the Castle Gate payroll of the Pleasant Valley Coal Company on April 21, 1897. During that same period Kid Curry, together with Flatnose George Curry, the Sundance Kid and several others, had attempted to hold up the bank at Belle Fourche, South Dakota, were pursued, captured and escaped from the jail at Deadwood. It was obvious that Cassidy (with the help of Elza Lay, a brilliant strategist) had won.

Following the battle at Hole-in-the-Wall between law officers and the Hole-in-the-Wall Gang, the gang made a hasty exodus to

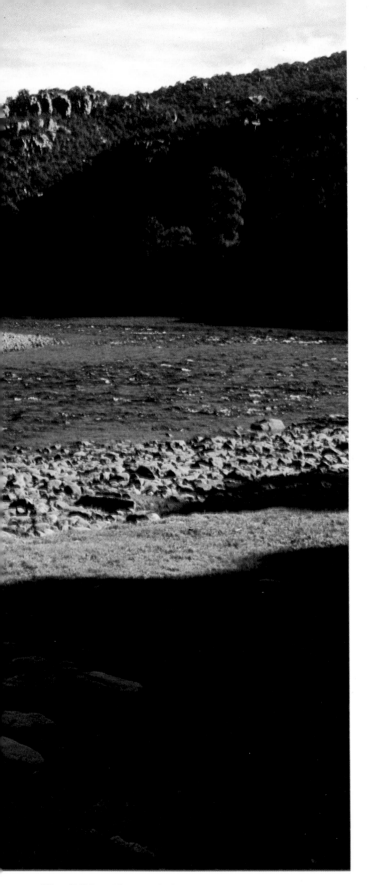

Kim Whitesides and the author saddle up at Little Hole where the opening sequence of Jeremiah Johnson *was filmed.*

George Wetherill was tried and convicted on several counts of murder by a jury in Canon City, Colorado. The townspeople came out on December 4, 1888 to watch him hanged from a telephone pole.

Brown's Park in August, 1897, and the rendezvous with Butch Cassidy. Local newspapers reported that the Hole-in-the-Wall Gang numbered seventy-five men, and they were an impressive force as they passed through Wyoming towns on their way south.

All that remains of Cassidy Point now is a large trench, excavated in front of the old cabin site, in which the men proposed to make a last stand if they were ever surrounded by the law.

Here, at the foot of Diamond Mountain in a small draw that led to the river, we stopped while Whitesides brewed up some herb tea

Elza Lay: Tall, handsome, and charming, he became Butch Cassidy's right-hand man. Known as "the educated outlaw," he planned most of the daring robberies executed by the Wild Bunch, and his brilliant schemes were widely admired.

Harvey Logan (standing) and Harry Longabaugh (The Sundance Kid) posed for this photograph taken about 1895.

Baggs, Wyoming in 1912. It was here in the Bull Dog Saloon that Newt Kelly and Tom Horn had a knife fight.

Dr. John Parsons's cabin was built in Brown's Park in 1874. It later became a popular shelter for men on the run, including Matt Warner and Butch Cassidy.

(which was beginning to grow on me) with a few raisins, sunflower seeds and almonds thrown in on the side. It had been a long day with a lot of riding and a great deal to think about, so we decided to pitch camp. The moon was almost full and it was clear, promising another cold night.

The next morning we feasted on Whitesides's natural health formula and pancakes and bacon—again, with lots of coffee. Interestingly, Whitesides consistently ate both his own natural concoctions and our more traditional menu.

The horses were beginning to act as if we were impositions and were more and more difficult to prod. Terry Minger was trying valiantly to be a good sport by hiding the

A view of Brown's Hole, Utah from Jesse Ewing Canyon.

Dr. John Parsons.

In 1971, just three days before the Department of Fish and Game was about to take down the cabin, Kerry and Marie Allen and others got it placed on the State Historical Register. This was a rare victory in the Utah-Colorado-Wyoming border country where the value of such preservation has not been publicized.

As we walked through the debris and high grass surrounding the place, I couldn't help but think how many of these old sites that might now be considered monuments have either been destroyed, or buried by development, or have simply rotted away, weathered and neglected, away from the caring eyes of those interested in preserving a piece of our past. The architecture, born of the genuine need for survival, was sound and the notched logs that form the structure are still in place. The cabin has only enough space to live and function in. It was an appealing sight and a sad one. In back of the cabin were stacked some aged boards and posts. This rubble was evidence of how little value is placed on the past. It reminded me of our society's penchant for discarding older citizens with only token care and small tolerance.

I looked back toward Diamond Mountain to Cassidy Point, the old Crouse Ranch, Parsons' cabin, and wondered what would

pain in his lower regions, but gave himself away by posting a lot. We nicknamed him "Lord Minger."

We dropped into a flat area to the north near the river where we saw the remains of an old cabin and several surrounding shacks in varying stages of decay. This, said Bob Allen, was the old Doc Parsons cabin.

The Parsons family were among the first settlers in Brown's Park around 1858. The cabin was constructed in 1874, along with smelter for ore mined in the region. Doc Parsons died in 1881 and is buried near this cabin, as is his granddaughter. His son-in-law raised and trained pure-bred horses and sold them to the outlaws. In 1882 the cabin was vacated and used from time to time as a shelter for the outlaws. Matt Warner lived there for a while with his wife, as did Butch Cassidy, Elza Lay and others.

become of them. Ignorance and the Bureau of Land Management may doom the entire area to memory and legend. Around Vernal, Utah, the Diamond Mountain, the Red Canyon, in almost every spot that is not forest or Park Service land, the sprawling hand of the developer can be seen: mineral companies ravaging the land for oil and gas development and real estate agents in dark glasses glibly stating from their portable trailers: "You can own a second home here on Diamond Flats where the outlaws roamed."

Back at the Allen Ranch, Bill Allen gave us instructions on how to get to Little Hole, originally called Little Brown's Hole since it was a miniature of Brown's Hole, or Brown's Park as it is called today. From the late 1850s to 1920 this was a refuge for the gangs of "Mexican Joe" Herrera, Hank Golden and Tom Crowley, as well as the Red Sash Gang and the Wild Bunch. It was here that Harry A. Longabaugh worked as a horse wrangler for Cleophas J. Dowd, who gave him the name "Sundance Kid."

Allen told us there were two ways we could get to Little Hole. One was to go back up the canyon by which we had entered the Park, swing around the mountains some sixty miles to the north and come down to Little Hole through a community called Dutch John at the southern end of the Flaming Gorge Dam. The other was to hike ten miles or so over a pass through a narrow niche called Devil's Hole and drop down to Little Hole from the south. It was decided that Kim Whitesides and I would hike it and the others would take supplies and horses around the long way. Terry Minger decided to go in the Red Lemon to give his backside a rest, although considering the shape of the car, this was unlikely.

It was close to 2:30 P.M. and the winter sun would soon die behind the mountains. A

Cleophas Dowd (1856–1898) lived many lives: priest, gunslinger, rancher, detective, United States marshal. He spoke seven languages and several Indian dialects. The other residents of Brown's Park admired him for his intelligence but were wisely cautious of his temperamental nature.

Bill Carver.

The LaSal Mercantile Co. of Moab, Utah
probably had as many outlaws as customers.

*Stagecoach stopped along the Price-Vernal
route through Utah.*

move in the wrong direction could lead us into a labyrinth of canyons and gulleys. There was a small moment of anxiety as Bob Allen and his father got into an argument over how long the hike was, and where the trail over the pass could be found. Bob said it was sixteen miles but his father thought it was closer to eight. We decided that the father had lived there longer and *his* memory should be relied upon so we would attempt the hike. The other concern on the route was the hunters. Dan Arensmeier warned us, "Be careful. Man has come into the forest." We had no intention of being targets, so Kim and I put on bright-colored neckerchiefs before we headed for the pass.

We hoped to meet the others at the first bend in the river at Little Hole by dark. It was hardly a plan that made us feel secure, but our apprehensions were soon submerged in the awesome beauty of the hike. It was good to be footloose and unencumbered by horse and pack. I felt a great energy and the uphill climb was festooned with pleasant diversions of natural interest. We followed a dry creek bed up through twisted piñon trees and huge rocks alive with lichen from the past. Great splashes of the orange growth stood out against the dark gray of the granite rock. From time to time we would pause and soak up the view and the fruits of the exercise. Not much was said. There was little to say, and Whitesides doesn't talk much anyway. We came across several plants that I couldn't

identify and I wondered if many people had ever taken this route. It seemed so virginal and untrampled by humanity.

After a while, we both had a nagging fear that the light would play out before there was any sure sign we were moving in the right direction. (Had Bob Allen been right after all?) Then through a niche in the rock we spotted the deep blue green of the river below. Knowing that the river was our best navigational source, we decided to drop down to its banks and follow its edge. The late afternoon sun was touching each bend in the river, casting it in a beautiful backlight. The river looked calm and green, like a fairy-tale illustration. We edged along the bank for two miles or so, then cliffs intercepted our path so we traversed by ledges from there on. Night was coming on as we dropped down to the Little Hole region.

It was a warm and nostalgic sight to me since we had filmed the opening sequence of *Jeremiah Johnson* at this spot and I remembered it well. In 1971 we had built an entire settlement for the film from historic photographs and had prevailed upon the studio to leave it there when we were finished, thinking it might be enjoyed by the citizens of neighboring Vernal and other communities as well as tourists. But the

Bureau of Land Management said it had no intention of maintaining it and tore it down before it could become "a public nuisance." So, where just a few years ago there had been a thriving Western town with a dock, post office, saloon and encampment, there was now just another bend in the river—a welcome sight nonetheless.

Incredibly, the others arrived at approximately the same time in one of those flukes of timing when it all works out. We celebrated the accuracy of Bill Allen's memory and then set about the final task of the day, which was fording the river to the other side where the old cabin sites were. This required some ingenuity, and since Ed Abbey was the river rat among us, he was elected to organize the crossing. We inflated an army surplus raft we had with us and decided that Ed and I would ride two horses across, pulling the raft loaded with supplies. We secured the raft by two ropes and attached them to our saddle horns.

The current was swift and the river was rising because of the floodgate-control operations at the dam that occur twice daily. I remembered a sunken sand-and-rock bridge and we headed for it. The horses obviously thought this was the latest in a long line of punishments as the water foamed up around their shoulders. Some

time ago I had learned from an old rancher friend the knack of navigating a river on horseback, particularly in a swift current. The trick was to go slow, keep an even pace and make sure the horse's head was held up and pointed in a slightly upstream direction. If the horse's head was allowed to drift to a position perpendicular to the opposite bank or go under the water, he would panic. Realizing this was something he wasn't supposed to be able to do, he would flounder and possibly overturn and trample you in a mad effort to gain a purchase point with his hooves. In that case, if the water was deep enough, you could both drown.

Although the stream here wasn't all that deep, the horses did begin to paw for footing and there were a few tense moments. I could see by Ed's expression that his faith in the venture was waning. Water was hitting the raft broadside, but we got across before it could swamp the horses as they stomped and lurched to the safety of the bank in a spray of water and rock. This maneuver was repeated twice until all supplies and riders were across. The final trip was with Arlinka and Dan. Dan was having a high old time, and while Arlinka was not quite sure at first, she finally got caught up in Dan's enjoyment and joined in the lark.

Ed gave me his horse and he floated the raft down to the bend a mile below, where we would camp. It was great fun, and by the time we had settled bedrolls and fed the horses and built a fire, dinner was a

Rafting down the Green River at Little Hole, Utah.

prime delight. We had caught some trout from the river and Arlinka made her magic kitchen with lemon, oil and a touch of Kim Whitesides' herbal seasoning. There were no pans, so she soaked the fish in butter, pressed them with almonds and wrapped them in tinfoil.

Arlinka's impact upon the group had been a subtle one. She had a quiet, unobtrusive, utilitarian presence that grew by increments into a glow of warmth and attractiveness. She made no fuss, no demands that ran counter to the flow of action, showed no remorse at failed plans. And she was there—always—on time, eager, ready, sporty and forward looking, searching out the optimistic part of any troubled situation. Because she rests so well with herself there was never a suggestion of disapproval of another person. You didn't notice all this at first. You became aware only after a while of an enduring good nature that transformed depression into hope, of a pragmatic wisdom that could be implemented with surprising skills—skills that kept unfolding with no announcement. I began to cherish her good will and strength and that night I had to admit to a chauvinistic appreciation of her outdoor commissary.

Ed Abbey cooked chili and we washed it down with beer. By the time we had finished

Tom McCarty, the son of a doctor, became an outlaw and accompanied Butch Cassidy and Matt Warner on many holdups.

dinner, given hay to the horses and settled down with "cowboy coffee," the moon had come up. It was incredible. Full and bright. And with no pollution haze to mar its glow, the entire area was soon bathed in a light blue. All was still and the only sound was the crackle of the fire and the steady roar of the river nearby. Jupiter and Saturn were out together and visible in the same sky, a treat for the senses and a tonic to any harassed soul. It was the best night by far. Kim talked about a method of growing beans at home, letting them sprout lightly and then cooking them. He was really into it, but no one cared. Everyone was tired but it was difficult to go to sleep. The thought of wasting such an idyllic moment seemed criminal. So we all lay awake for a while each lost in his or her own thoughts. I thought about the horses tethered in seclusion, about the hike over the pass, the sound of the river, the detailing of forms that a bright moon brings, of stars and galaxies and legends and how perfect it all seemed. Everything in harmony—a moment in time and place one dreams about. I wondered about the future of the Park. A natural resource of history threatened by the Bureau of Land Management and its churning of piñon trees, its razing of old cabin sites and by man's encroachment on these fine old relics—our need to push ahead, sometimes at any cost. But these unsettling thoughts were washed away finally by the perfection of the moment.

A beautiful morning, cold and clear. The trees were losing their leaves so one could see as far as the eye allowed. Dan remarked on what a perfect spot this was for an outlaw stronghold—plenty of deer and elk, the best fishing anywhere (the river is literally jumping with trout) and good water. In the old days loose railroad ties from the rail construction up above would float down the river. Knowing that if they could recover these they would not have to cut down cedars for building material, the outlaws would tie a rope across the river at a shallow point and let it drag on the water to catch many of the ties in a jam. With these ties they constructed their homes. Only Tom Crowley's cabin is still in existence today, and it, too, is in danger of destruction. It was constructed in 1869 and has seen many characters since then, including Cleophas J. Dowd, the famed gunman of Brown's Park; Matt Warner; Butch Cassidy (who lived in it while constructing his own cabin a few hundreds yards away); the McCartys and the Sundance Kid. In this cabin a man named Mexican Charlie was knifed for cheating at cards and his body lies in a secluded grave a few yards to the south.

Now the old Crowley and Cassidy cabins are little more than memories that dance in the head. All that's left of Butch's place, which he used shortly before he left for South America and was his last real residence, is some rocks and a few upright boards with trees growing up through them. It's off the beaten track and no one would ever see it if he didn't know what to look for.

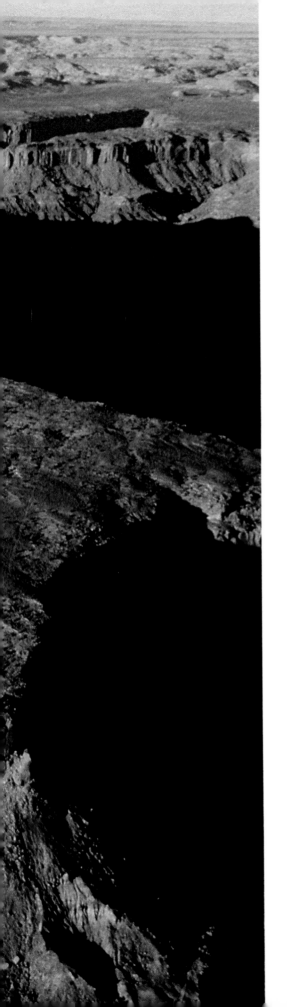

ROBBERS ROOST

The next way station on the Outlaw Trail was Robbers Roost. Upon leaving Brown's Park, the trail is covered over by highway. At Dutch John at the west end of the Park, the Green River, which flows cold and torrential from its source in the mountains, is dammed up to form Flaming Gorge, a boating and fishing paradise for local Utahans and their neighbors.

We had to travel by four-wheel to Vernal, where the trail drops directly south through parched canyon and finally emerges into the dry, desolate and forbidding magnificence of Canyonlands, Utah. We said good-bye to the Allens, father and son, and headed up along the Manila Highway, which hugs the southwest side of the Gorge. It seemed strange to suddenly be moving so quickly in comparison to the previous days. Scenery and miles sped by in a blur. One could imagine what the old-timers must have felt living through the accelerating phases of transportation over the last sixty years—from horse to train to car to jet. Can the time be far off when we will be traveling by airwave? I had started to think of this on a few occasions while lying in the outback staring up at the sprawling universe. The night sky was alive with shooting objects (many of them man's inventions), orbiting in a frenzied heat to leave this galaxy and move outward. Traffic in the sky, the contrails crisscrossing each other in a kind of heavenly tic-tac-toe.

There is a lot of history buried beneath the tonnage of water in the Gorge. We were told that many cabins, caves, gravesites—in fact, whole homesteads and entire towns—had been inundated by the damming. No attempt had been made to relocate, resurrect or simply preserve any of this. It had been gracelessly crushed by the stream of progress and now lies rotting in the sediments of geologic time.

On the way to Vernal we passed through Sheep Creek Canyon, a paradise that appears suddenly and looks like what one expects to find at the end of a rainbow. It is filled with yellow aspens, green fields and red and black rocks rising like the spires of a cathedral. The original Outlaw Trail can still be seen here as it winds up behind the stables to higher country.

We stopped to look at the cabin and grave of Cleophas Dowd, one historical site that has been preserved. Dowd was murdered here in his stables by a Mexican sheepherder. He had been involved with Tom Horn in the Johnson County War in 1892. He and Horn had some evidence against George Dunning, a turncoat outlaw who had hired a man named Reaser to kill Dowd. Dowd had been laid up all winter with a bullet wound in the groin following an argument with his brother, and Reaser had been hired on as a "hand." In the spring of 1898 Reaser snuck up on Dowd in the stables and shot him twice in the head. He then fired a bullet in the wall above his head so he would be able to claim self-defense. The bullet holes are visible in the old run-down shack that was once the stables, and the two graves are on a mound behind the cabin.

Dowd was a bizarre character. He had been born of Irish Catholic parents in an old mission in San Francisco in 1856. He alternately studied at the mission and ran away to his father's ranch in Marin County. For a while he took up with a gang on the Barbary Coast but returned to the mission to be ordained a Catholic priest on his twenty-first birthday. He then strapped on guns, shot up the town of Sausalito and escaped as a fugitive to Brown's Park, Utah. Through the years he maintained relations with outlaws in that region while working as a Pinkerton detective, stockman, deputy, United States marshal and railroad detective.

It was Dowd who established the portion of the Outlaw Trail behind his ranch. In the dugout (which still stands) was a door hidden behind a cupboard leading into a tunnel through Red Hill, which opened into a corral at the bottom of the trail where horses were kept ready. This convenient escape route was used by many of the outlaws.

One is curious whether, under different circumstances, Dowd's splendid ingenuity might not have bred a leader with immense social impact. Had he applied his inventive mind and various skills in other directions, there is no telling what turn our social history might have taken. And there were so many enterprising souls like him—all, but for the grace of God, financial wizards, inventors or corporate barons. I had become increasingly intrigued by the many outlaws who had demonstrated wit and brains unmatched by any but the most brilliant in legitimate society. We have an abiding impression of the outlaw as a low-life renegade, a violent fool who lived off luck and the gun. We view him as one of society's misbegotten who had to be hunted down like an animal by morally superior men in white hats. But it was not so. In truth, the line between the "good guy" and the "bad guy" in the West was often blurred, and many of the outlaws, in spite of their errant and often violent natures, were men of extraordinary skill and cunning, who by comparison made the lawmen look pathetic.

We continued on up through fantastic geological formations of warped and folded rock. Signs of nature's upheaval are prominent in these mountains. The rock colors changed fantastically from red and white to yellow and black. We came down on the other side to pine meadowed flats where mountain breezes blew the tall grasses like water rippling in a lake.

We drove down to Vernal, Utah through more magnificent country of unfolding variety—great formations of topography—the oldest on earth. It is here that the great dinosaur remains from the Jurassic age were located years ago. In the distance the Colorado plateau stretched across the horizon, so lean and graceful, encompassing such incredible space, in perfect harmony with the sky. It is rankling to imagine its certain fate at the hands of oil shale and other kinds of development.

Down along Nine Mile Canyon now. A narrow downhill shaft, five times longer than nine miles, winds through lower foliage and much rock and shale. It is a parched and somewhat desolate canyon filled with signs of a once-thriving civilization of ancient hunters and gatherers. Pictographs and petroglyphs of the Anasazi Indians can be found on the canyon walls. We stopped to watch the play of two gopher hawks against the skyline. Then at the bottom of the canyon we came across a series of ranches and old cabins set in a pleasant surprise of rich and abundant green. This area was part of the old trail used

These two men seem to be enjoying the contents of their jug.

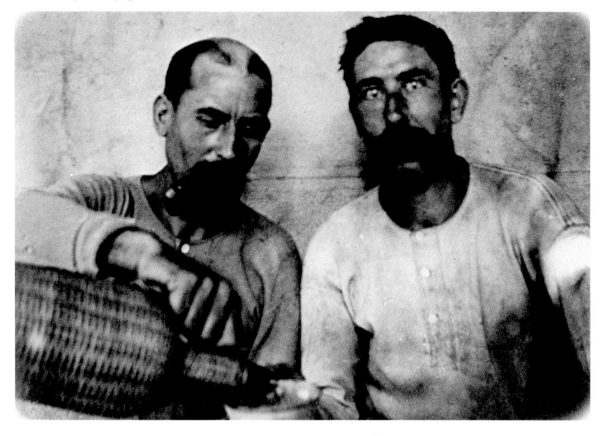

by Butch Cassidy on his southward flight through the country he knew so well.

I stopped to talk to a rancher standing in a field, working on a bruised piece of equipment. He was leathery and squint-eyed from so much time outdoors. I was unprepared for the hostility my questioning aroused.

"How long have I been here? Too damn long."

"It's very beautiful," I offered.

"Yeah? Well, I tell ya, you can have it. You give me half of what I got in those cows out back there and you can have 'em."

"Things aren't good?"

"Ain't nothin' here but dust and rocks and some starvin' cows. Let me outta here and up to Minnesota. That's the only place left where a man can make a livin' farmin' or ranchin'. I can make more standin' on my head in Minnesota than I can here."

"What's wrong?" I asked.

"There's no water, no one has the money to develop it for ranchin'. All they's interested in is buyin' up mineral rights for power and real estate. We're gettin' starved out."

"Who's doing it?"

"Lots of people. People comin' from the outside. I'm not from here myself. . . I come down from Wyoming a few years back. But these new people, they're not ranchers,

At Sheep Creek Canyon black and red rocks rise like cathedral spires out of groves of yellow aspens.

they're from the city. They land here in helicopters, buy a bunch of ground and leave. They wear suits mostly . . . and buy up land by the thousands of acres. You wanna tell me they're interested in ranchin'? Hell."

He was standing here, one foot balanced on the blade of a tractor plow, in dust-and-oil-caked overalls, wiping his hands over and over in a grease-stained cloth. The gesture seemed to bear something more than personal hygiene. It was a gesture of bitterness, an effort to cleanse frustrations. I asked him if he owned the land we were on.

"No, just sharecroppin' you might say. I own all this equipment, but I'm leasin' the ground. Equipment's costin' me more to keep up than I can make off the cows and the ground here is dryin' up 'cause of the drought."

"What about that ranch I just passed?" I asked. "That looked green and beautiful, even had some old relic cabins on it."

"Yeah, but ain't nothin' bein' done with it. It's just sittin' until they decide to develop the minerals here. Some outfit outta New York come in here a couple of years ago and bought close to a million acres, and that's part of it. The original family moved out—what was left of 'em."

As we continued on I thought that this was the real plight of the ranchers in the area. They often don't see the beauty of their surroundings because they feel economically blocked by those surroundings and therefore resent them.

As we slowly rode through the canyon we met others, less angry, though very often in the same plight. The difference was these ranchers had kept their pride despite the hardships of the drought. Members of the fifth generation to live here, they were determined to hang on, and do whatever they had to to survive. They were owners of still working ranches. But the prevailing mood was one of resignation to the changing times.

Nine Mile Canyon eventually runs out onto the flats of the lower Colorado Plateau. Here the vista is wide and diverse. To the east are the buckled citadels of an area called the Book Cliffs—great erosions caused by runoff from the higher mountains. To the south begins an arid swirling maze of formations called Canyonlands, a great yawning space of gulleys, rock formations and dried river beds. Heatwaves quiver above its surface and the view seems endless and forbidding. Warm pastel colors of the land are reflected in the cloud formations above.

There is probably no other spot in the United States save possibly the Grand Canyon, where the awesome beauty of nature's violent erosion is so apparent. One does not feel the presence of any

animal, let alone man.

On the north edge of this space is the small town of Green River, once a major intersection in the sparse network of towns that stretched from the Midwest to the West Coast. Once a cattle and mining town that drew people from great distances, it has now shrunken to small-town proportions in comparison to other Western towns. It sits on the edge of nature's abyss, lying in wait for an energy and industrial boom that seems inevitable. It is an attractive town in contrast to others, caught in the transition between what once was and what is surely to be.

One can find general delivery stores and dry goods—stores where you can go in and find just about anything to suit a need, but stores that are still privately owned. This is set against signs of a more plastic age—the long string of dairy freeze and fast-food operations that have become endemic to America's taste buds.

We hooked up here with a man named A. C. Ekker and his father, Arthur, who would outfit our ride from this point on into more desolate country.

We had set a date to meet him at a Phillip's 66 gas station in the center of town. As we drove into this oasis and I saw the name Green River on a sign, I thought, "How many Green Rivers are there in the U.S.? How many states boast that name? Like the name Springfield, it seems to pop up everywhere."

A. C. Ekker is an energetic young man who runs an outfit called Outlaw Trails, Inc. His father, Arthur, was born down in the Roost area and has ranched it all his life. The Ekkers are a large pioneer family from the Green River, Hanksville and Emory County area in southern Utah. A.C. is a hard-working, hard-riding, hard-thinking ex-rodeo cowboy who suggests, more than anyone I've come across, the verve, strength, enthusiasm and enterprise attributed to the early settlers. In a sinking society of worn leather and tired spirits, he stands out as a leader—forward-looking, hopeful, suggesting the ability to bring it all together single-handedly. Outlaw Trails, Inc. venture is largely his doing and its maintenance and success his province.

He was going to be our guide for the most rugged segment of the trail ride, down through the treacherous and forbidding desolation of Canyonlands and the meandering canyons of such rivers as the Yampa and the Dirty Devil, and on the parched flats west of the confluence of the Green and Colorado rivers. These are areas where nature has displayed her temper, warping and twisting the land in violent configurations of spires, mesas, deep, dark canyons, rolling faults of rocks and gulleys and gulches, so dry and barren it appears man has never set foot in them.

Ekker, of course, knows this country well

The high desert country of southeastern Utah provided natural escape routes that threaded the canyon mazes

The birthplace of Butch Cassidy near Circleville, Utah.

and knows where the few springs are along the way. The area was ideal for the outlaw in this respect—no posse could ever seem to learn where the water holes were, while the outlaws, having memorized the routes through the region and the locations of the springs, would purposely lead the chase parties astray, usually to a dry back canyon. The lawmen would become disoriented, lose their way and often die of starvation or dehydration. For this reason the law seldom ventured into this savage land, and an outlaw would be safe for any length of time he chose to stay buried in its confusion.

Ekker had just returned from outfitting a group of hunters in Colorado and had lost patience with "greenhorns." No one of us was going to fall into that category if we could help it, but on close examination of Ekker, we could see it might be a test. There was something in A.C.'s attitude, his look, that said he thought we might be tenderfoots out on a joyride. That he might have to bring us down to size and show us a more realistic version of things. I thought Garvin and Curt Taylor had had similar feelings our first night on the trail, and I didn't blame any of them. I would have had the same pride in being genetically connected to the true West rather than to a movie or pulp book view of it, and I doubt I could have resisted the urge to test folks a bit either. There was excitement in this unspoken challenge. In his crisp, fast-moving, friendly manner, A. C. was promising some hard rides ahead.

We were joined here by Dan's wife, Sherry, who had been unable to start the trip with us. Needless to say, Arlinka, having been a minority of one up to this point, was thrilled. The new face was vibrant and attractive to the rest of us too, who by now were beginning to resemble a load of refugees from a war camp. In fact, "attractive" is the complete adjective for Sherry. She is a tall, smart, handsome, raven-haired woman who has a ready smile and a forgiving nature. With her keen coordination, easy manner and quiet dignity, she is the epitome of the Western woman—capable, enterprising and at home in the saddle. We threw around a few jokes about what she was in for, and she said she wouldn't miss it for the world.

At this, A. C. said, "Well then let's roll 'em out," and we saddled up and rode south to a section along the San Raphael Swell called Temple Junction.

Temple Junction is in need of a spirit. It is nothing more than a cinder-block foundation, some shattered boarding, a tin roof slid off to one side and a dry well. Bullet holes are everywhere. In these parts when something no longer shows signs of life it automatically becomes fair game for target practice. Here we headed due east for some twenty-five miles, into what must be one of the most desolate spots in the entire Southwest. A sign warns that you'd best take plenty of gas and water and have at least a jeep for transport; that you are now prey to desert fever, buzzards and exposure for the next hundred miles; and that outside of a ranger station forty miles to the east there is nothing—nothing but space and nature's carving. The sign said: "Proceed at own risk."

We made our way east across some of the most beautiful and varied expanses we had yet traveled. The space and late-afternoon amber sun made such a great display of energy and light that we stopped to digest it. It seemed here that we could see as far as was humanly possible. The old outlaws had had all this for free. I wondered if they had appreciated it or if they had taken such treasures for granted.

It was a day getting to the Ekker Ranch, which was mounted like a set in a Western movie against an unrelieved horizon. There was a bunkhouse, an old garage and a well, the main house with that great equalizer, the outhouse, just behind it, and two crude horse corrals and an old well-preserved

A. C. Ekker, "a hard-working, hard-riding, hard-thinking ex-rodeo cowboy," acted as guide across the rugged Robbers Roost territory.

tackhouse. The earth was that rare color of red—a fine mix of sand and clay, a sea of sage, sand and piñon peppered with junipers. The red color was reflected on the bottom edge of the clouds so that everywhere was the tint of red.

Arthur Ekker is a fine old hand. He has energy born as much from need as anything else, and at seventy-three, work and movement are ingrained in him. He is sandy-haired and leathery-skinned beyond belief and his eyes are folded into a permanent squint. He speaks in bursts of exclamations as though he had dozed off between thoughts and didn't want to get caught at it. He has a hearty, quick laugh that has a bit of mischievousness to it. Between crusty Art and his son one is easily intimidated.

General stores like this one were common in frontier towns.

162

Canyonland of southern Utah.

We helped the two men herd the horses into corrals, and washed up from well water in a pan and sat down to a real ranch dinner. Mrs. Ekker had come out to do the cooking, along with two wranglers who work for A.C. We had a delightful meal of fried chicken, biscuits (God, how I do love biscuits—I had fifteen), honey, carrots, beer, wine and talk, mostly from Arthur. As he told us the history of the Roost and the entire region, his constant, even patter and easy recall reminded me of Garvin Taylor.

Robbers Roost was the last and perhaps most unique of the three big way stations along the trail. This was desolate country and it was virtually impossible to follow a lead."

He told us how the outlaws would rustle their cattle into the Roost, which was a five-mile circular flat that had lookout points on all sides. The Roost is identifiable by two flat-topped buttes on the edge of the flat, facing east and north. It provided the outlaws with caves in which to store their weapons, bunkhouses, saloons and such "essentials" as disguised hollowed-out trees for the posting of letters and messages. Isolated from settlements by miles of desert and box canyons, it was almost inaccessible except to the few who knew the route, and many lawmen brave or foolish enough to penetrate the refuge were lost in the mazes or

perished from thirst. Because the outlaws knew where the vital springs were, they could survive.

It is forty miles to Hanksville to the west, fifty-five miles to Green River to the north and thirty miles to Dandy Crossing to the south. To the east are dried-up gulleys and pinnacle rocks leading to confusion.

The waterways that dissect this area are tributaries of the Green, San Raphael and Dirty Devil rivers. Here the outlaws had their choice of routes leading out. To the west, they could traverse the Angel Trail along the Dirty Devil River through Hanksville and on out to the Outlaw Trail; to the east and south, they could cross Horsethief Canyon and the "Maze" into Colorado and then south to Texas and Mexico. It was a fortressed triangle of deep canyons, rivers and mesas and perfectly suited the needs of the outlaws.

"Yep, ol' Butch was the best," Arthur said as he pried away with a toothpick in the darker regions of his mouth. (His slicked-down hair was his one concession to dinner-table formality.) "Plenty popular in these parts. Born not far from here . . . over to Beaver. Took good care of the ranchers. My mom and dad remembered him well. Ya know, he's the one that started this whole Pony Express business in robbin' banks and trains. First ones here, though, was the McCartys. Ol' Matt Warner and Butch learned from them. Used to bring stolen herds of cattle in from Nevada. No one could follow 'em. Too damn tough. When the coast was clear, they'd take 'em up on the Henry Mountains and fatten 'em. That'd be about 1872. Butch didn't show up till around 1885 or so. Ol' Cap Brown was here too. Used to steal herds out in western Utah, bring 'em through the Roost, shake the law, and trail 'em over to Colorado to sell to the miners. Fact, he's likely the one that built the corrals over to Twin Corral flats. Every trail in and outta here is the original one carved by the early ol' boys."

Kerry Boren chimed in on his automatic history pilot, reeling off more information: "They used to live in sandstone caves or crude cabins of twisted cedar. In fact, my great-grandfather was hidden out in the Roost by Butch Cassidy in 1886 to avoid the U.S. marshals for polygamy."

We talked of many things: the early settlers, the Green River, the spirits the outlaws believed haunted the place.

Arthur said how honorable Butch had been—always leaving something for the ranchers, taking care of them in return for their help. And he always kept his word. For their part, the ranchers would deny having seen him at all. It was a day when a piece of paper wasn't necessary to an agreement. The rule of word—what if you broke it?

"Well," said Arthur, "then someone

The author's party sits down to dinner at the Ekker ranch.

would show up sooner or later and put a bullet in you to square the deal."

We slept out under the desert stars that hang so low. It was the last night of the full moon. The air was balmy and the only sounds were the occasional stirrings of the horses in the corral.

The next day we woke up to a cloudless azure sky. The Henry Mountains, sixty miles to the west, were ablaze with the first light.

We had another hearty meal (the Ekkers had been up a long while doing chores) and then rode out along the Angel Trail. We searched for the wild horses A.C. said were in the area, Dan and I chasing a rabbit along the way. It felt good to really stretch out over these plains, to cut loose and give free rein to the horse. We raced along, the horses' hooves clipping the top of the sage and pounding through the red clay. I lost my hat but didn't stop for it because it felt so good to be moving. It was lost to some future prospector or cow with an appetite for variety.

Even with views up to seventy and eighty miles we couldn't see the wild horses, but the search was fun. We headed over to Horse Thief Canyon, some fifteen miles east of the ranch, alternately flushing ravens, rabbits and idle cows from their nesting spots. At the edge of the canyon A.C., who never slowed below a trot, pointed to something in the sand. It was a flint-chipping camp, a place where a thousand years ago Indians gathered flint and chert and worked them

Despite his seventy-odd years, Arthur Ekker puts in a full day in the saddle. His bloodied hands suggest the type of work involved in running a cattle ranch.

Robert Leroy Parker (Butch Cassidy) spent his boyhood on a ranch outside of Circleville, Utah. He learned the art of cattle rustling at an early age and soon became familiar with hideouts such as Robbers Roost.

Henry Rhodes (Bub) Meeks, Jr., the son of a prosperous rancher in Utah, joined the Wild Bunch when they passed through his territory. He was arrested for his part in a bank robbery at Montpelier, Idaho and sent to a state penitentiary.

This stump is what remains of the "Post Office Tree" where outlaws left messages and letters.

Disgruntled guards and miners of the Pleasant Valley Coal Company in Castle Gore, Utah gathered on the scene moments after Butch Cassidy and Elza Lay made off with their payroll on April 21, 1897.

The author and Arthur Ekker work on saddle bags.

into arrowheads. We stopped and combed through the sand looking for arrowheads and the chipping stones used to carve the heads. We found three or four and packed them away for souvenirs. To this day no one has been able to figure out how these Indians worked the flint into arrowheads. The skills are buried along with their civilization in the shifting sands.

By now the wind had come up and the temperature had dropped. The sand felt like a hundred pinpricks on our skin and we discovered how really nothing can keep the sand out in a wind. We spotted some horses but they were stray ranch horses, so we settled for driving them hard back to the corral four miles away. By now the weather was changing drastically, the sky

A.C. Ekker, whose spirit recalls the pride and individualism of the Old West's heroes, here shows off his skill at roping steers.

Flatnose George Curry.

flatness and bundled up for the night. I was now using my saddle for a pillow, and I could feel the chill of the leather on my neck. Thank God I had negotiated a different sleeping bag from the one I had started with. In about an hour a wind came from the north and blew out the fire. There was such a desperate feeling of emptiness that it bordered on despair. No one mentioned what we all were thinking—that this was as far away from any road as we had been, some fifty miles or so. The darkness, the encompassing gloom, the emptiness made the inside of the sleeping bag seem warm and comforting, and those things that are magnified when you're enclosed in a small place—the sound of your own breathing, the awareness of your own presence—gave solace in the ambient loneliness.

t around six in the morning I awoke to find five inches of fresh snow covering my sleeping bag. Fortunately snow does have insulating qualities, but the *idea* made me cold. As beautiful as the landscape had been the day before, glazed in red, it was equally so today. But it was of a different variety, a great salt flat stoked by the crowns of green junipers. The sky was gray and even and *cold* was the word. It felt cold and looked cold.

Out of some concern and slight

blackening and the cold coming on. Because of the open space and flatness it felt like being on a ship just before a storm at sea. There's one thing about the windchill factor: once it sets in, you are finally and firmly *cold*.

That night there were no stars, just a blank darkness. Everyone hung by the fire as long as possible, somehow sensing that the oppressive low in the air signaled an ominous turn. Like animals rushing for cover before a storm, we all scattered to areas as secure as could be found in this open

apprehension, I guess, we ate a huge breakfast, saddled up and headed out for the Roost flats where the real outlaw stronghold had been and Butch Cassidy's hideout cave still exists. As we rode along, bones as brittle as ice shards, the gray oppressive stillness suddenly lifted like fog at noon. The air turned blue and frosty and everywhere was true white with color in it. It was revitalizing and we went wild.

A.C. had spotted the wild horses we had been looking for the previous day and we took out after them as if there were no other task and no tomorrow. We ran the horses to near exhaustion, not letting up, skimming along the top of the fresh snow, the horses in the lead kicking up a roostertail of white powder. After the night's sleep and the shot of adrenaline the cold had given us, we felt we could go forever. It was the longest I had ever ridden full-out and it felt good. At first you worry about chuck holes and exposed bedrock or juniper root, but then, in the ecstasy of movement free and all-out, you soon forget these concerns and give in to the moment.

We spotted the horses. The obvious leader was a beautiful buckskin stallion with the customary thick neck and a tail that fell to the ground. He led the others just a step ahead of us until we surrounded them three miles away at the base of a mesa. Our horses quivered with fatigue and excitement and the stallion's eyes were wide-alert and wild. Amidst the threat there was a feeling of play to all this, and I think the wild horse sensed it. In any case, after a good look we let them go and they ran away to the south, led by this untamed Pegasus. I couldn't deny the feeling of envy this sight provoked.

As I looked around, it seemed that I could see forever, as the saying goes. There were no parameters; the distance was so extreme and clear that you felt you had never seen before. The eye in this day and age is not accustomed to being asked to see more than a short distance, and usually there is so much to look at—buildings, people, cars, wires, windows, signs, billboards and lights—that it blights the senses. But here in this uncommon, virgin stretch of space with no boundary save a lone horse running wild in its center, I was overwhelmed. I felt lucky, lucky to see this, lucky to be *able* to see it. There is no way of knowing the exact impact a moment like that has on the psyche—but it can't be bad.

It was about ten miles to the Roost and down into a small cut where Butch Cassidy's

rock and cave were. The clear day was so cold that frostbite became a real threat. A wind was coming up and it increased the windchill factor as it whipped unblocked across the wide expanse. The worst thing about chill is the near impossibility of getting rid of it. The point is to avoid it. We stopped by Butch's rock and built a midday fire to cook lunch and get warm. Despite the cold everyone was very up—the ride had been exhilarating.

Arthur Ekker described the history of the spot. The rock chimneys still standing belonged to a man named J. D. Buhr, an English tailor who came to this country to cure his chronic asthma and settled at the Granite Ranch at the foot of the Henry Mountains. He idolized Butch and the other outlaws somewhat and spent a good deal of time at the Roost where, because of his asthma, he was known as "Wheezing" Buhr. Buhr was the prototype for the Englishman in Zane Grey's classic *Robbers' Roost*.

The original corral is still there and we put our horses in it while we ate. With the rocks like red sentinels behind us, the Dirty Devil Canyon below us, and a view of the Henry Mountains seventy-five miles away, everyone got high on space and air. We were fifteen miles from our campsite and once again we were made aware of the toughness of the people who had settled here. I looked at us all around the fire, gloved, jacketed, hunched over for warmth, and then at A.C. and his father working with the saddles,

collecting wood without gloves, seemingly oblivious of the elements. "You have no choice," said Art Ekker.

Afterward we circled the entire Roost area to see the various remnants of the outlaw society. Cassidy's camp was the center of all activity in the region. Even people who weren't considered outlaws, but were friends of Cassidy's, came to the camp to play poker and enter into horse races with the sporty members of the gang. It is said that Butch was the most amiable of all the Western outlaws, as much a fun lover as anything else, and there has been no evidence to disprove this.

The company of women had been most welcome at the Roost and many became the wives of Wild Bunch members. Ella Butler, Millie Nelson, Maude Davis (wife of Elza Lay) and the mysterious Etta Place (the Sundance Kid's girlfriend) were among the women there.

Kerry Boren informed us at this point that he was about to co-author a book on the outlaws with the son-in-law of Etta Place, who lives in Oklahoma. I told him that to my knowledge no one ever knew much about Etta Place, a fascinating person whose whereabouts after a certain point could not be traced. Kerry said that actually he knew a great deal about her from his own research

A stagecoach at the Robbers Roost station in 1885.

and the research of other historians.

It seems that Etta Place was born circa 1874, the daughter of the Honorable George Capel and the granddaughter of Arthur Algernon Capel, sixth Earl of Essex. Her father was killed before 1892 near Tombstone, Arizona, and Etta was practically raised by the outlaws with whom her father had associated. They even paid for her education. She had been living in the bordello district of San Antonio, Texas, when Butch Cassidy and his friends, including the Sundance Kid, brought her to Utah where she stayed with a Mormon family for a year or so. She then attended a teacher's college in the East and taught school for about one year in Telluride, Colorado, before joining Butch at Robbers Roost in 1895. The next part of her story has been documented fairly well in historic accounts and films. She traveled with Butch Cassidy and the Sundance Kid to New York and then Bolivia. The Sundance Kid brought her back to Denver and then returned to South America in 1909. Not much is known about her after that, though there are many versions of the rest of her story. Kerry says he believes she had a long life and had at least one daughter who died in 1971. "But," said Ed Abbey, "no one knows for sure, do they?"

We had to jog our horses along at a good clip to get to camp before dark. We had traveled close to thirty miles that day and my body was aware of it. The air was clean from

the snow and there were crystals everywhere. Now and then we spotted rabbit or coyote tracks. Clouds were coming on again and picking up reflections of purple, gold and red. Men had once traveled like this most of the time over even rougher terrain, covering even greater distances, because they had to. I asked Arthur Ekker if he remembered those times.

"Sure, when I was a kid, horse was the only way you could get around—car won't

Etta Place, granddaughter of the Earl of Essex, was a member of the Wild Bunch, and girlfriend of the Sundance Kid.

do you any good in these parts. Used to be five times as many horses in the area, good horses. Horse-tradin' business was a rich one. Steal a horse and you was a marked man . . . like takin' a man's gun away from him. You could find loads of wild herds round these flats and the mesas over to the foot of the Henrys—quarter horses, lot of purebreds. Ain't nothin' now. Hardly any horses left. No use for 'em."

he sunset was so beautiful no one wanted to quit for camp. Considering the time in the saddle and the amount of hard riding, we were gluttons for punishment. We warmed frozen appendages by a fire, beat frozen boots against rocks, drank herb tea, and listened to A.C. and his father talk more about the area, then and now. Arthur Ekker dominated the conversation.

On rustling: "Used to strip the skin back on the old brand of a cow and put a new one in. Most of the rustlers who came from Texas starting changin' brands . . . fast way to get into the cattle business."

On Butch Cassidy: "When I was a kid we were told never to ask questions when a stranger came to town. Agreement was no one would talk. We kids never knew nothin'. Our folks knew but they'd never say. Lotsa folk round these parts believe he never died in Bolivia. I never saw him, but a fella named

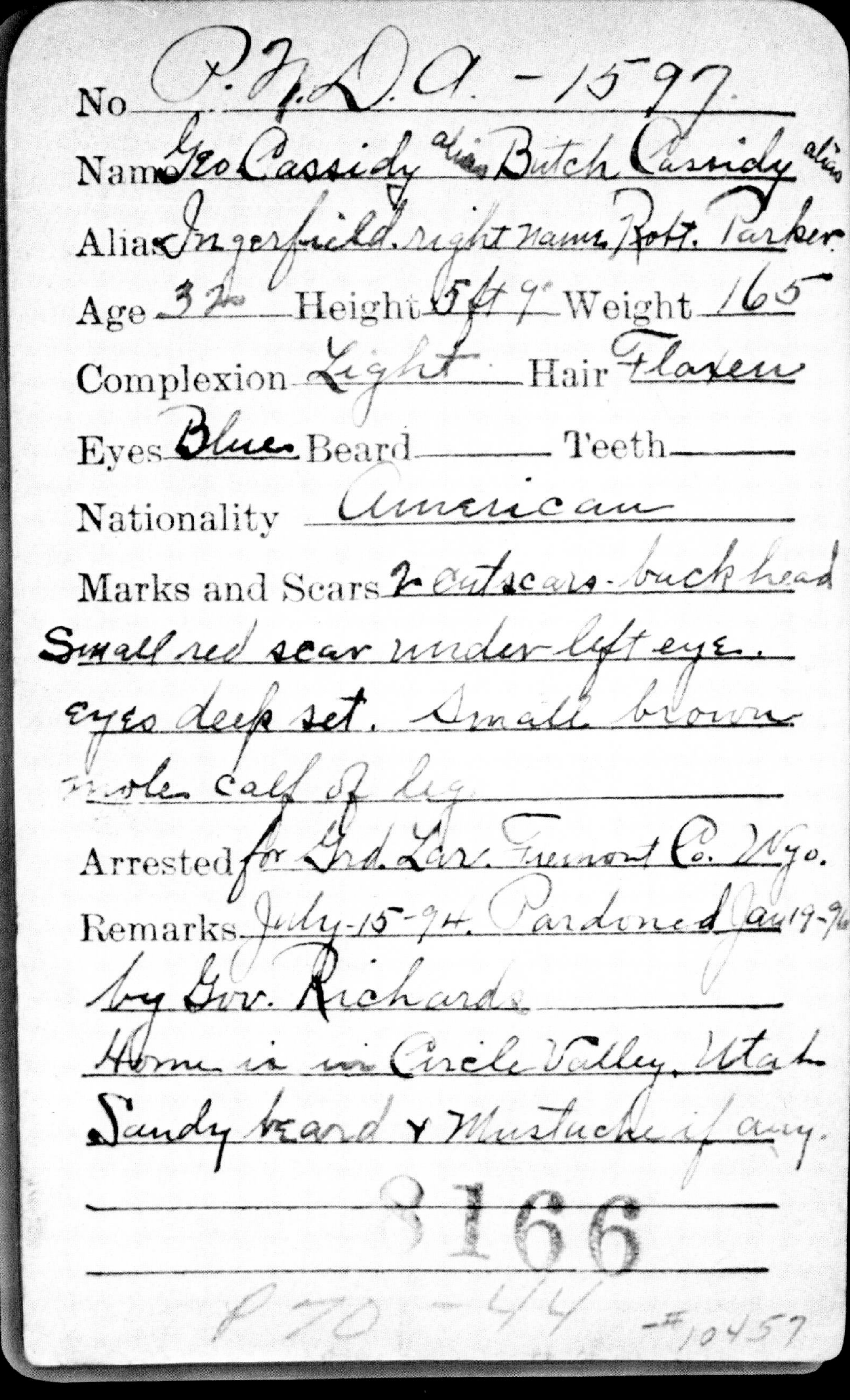

No _P.N.D.A. - 1597._

Name _Geo Cassidy_ alias _Butch Cassidy_ alias

Alias _Ingerfield. right name Robt. Parker_

Age _32_ Height _5 ft 9"_ Weight _165_

Complexion _Light_ Hair _Flaxen_

Eyes _Blue_ Beard _____ Teeth _____

Nationality _American_

Marks and Scars _2 cut scars. buck head_

Small red scar under left eye.

eyes deep set. Small brown

moles calf of leg

Arrested _for Grd. Lar. Fremont Co. Wyo._

Remarks _July-15-94. Pardoned Jan 19-96_

by Gov. Richards

Home is in Circle Valley. Utah

Sandy beard & Mustache if any.

8166

_P70 - 44   #10457_

This photograph of Mike Steele who grew up in Wayne County, Utah, has often been erroneously used as an image of Butch Cassidy.

Whiting from over to Hanksville who used to take supplies out here to the Roost for Butch, claimed he seen him in the twenties."

On the outlaw legends: "There's no real way to know other'n what you've seen or what your dad or ma tell you. I talk to you and you tell me a big windy, and then the next guy he tell me another windy—Christ, you get disgusted. Some stories was right and others couldn't be."

On his youth: "First time I took this Outlaw Trail I was seven or eight. Helped push a bunch of cows through here, up the steep section from the Dirty Devil on over to Moab 'cross Dead Man Point and Horseshoe

Canyon. Used to drive livestock all over here. Brought 'em down from Green River over from Hanksville and then south to New Mexico. In the old days people were tougher. Why, the people that lived over in Hanksville had to ride horses seventy-five miles to Green River to get the only doctor in the area. By the time you got there you was either dead or well. Undertaker did a hell of a lot of business. Later on, I used to move out here in the spring, leave wife and kids in Green River to school, and they'd move back for summer, then again for the holidays in winter. Kids had to help me work the ranch both winter and summer."

This corral built by outlaws before the turn of the century still stands today at Robbers Roost.

The *Outlaw Trail* riders travel across the plateau of Robbers Roost after the first snowfall of the season. The Henry Mountains loom in the background.

On Brigham Young: "He was a pretty good manager—arts, engineerin', city plannin'. Hoped for more out of the southern part of the state than what he got, though . . . wanted it to be another Dixie."

On land values and the Bureau of Land Management: "Oh, I get along okay with the Bureau. They came along and cut the land up pretty good. Don't feel it's worth that much. Families used to have more land here. People fought a lot with 'em at first. But it's okay now. Trouble is, they don't listen to no one. Not me, not anyone. We've lived here two or three generations. We've seen the land dryin' up. There used to be lots of antelope and wild horses and deer and cows and wild ducks and the like ya can't find now. Used to put up two hundred and ten ton of hay in a season. Now you can't get ten ton. Used to rain every other day or so in summer—a man could put up a good livin'—now there's no water. Moisture's been fallin' off. Have to cut down livestock as the water falls off. Ya see, most of the water round here is well and spring . . . runs through fissures in the rock, but there is definitely less. Springs are dryin' up. Ranches aren't practical here anymore, but the BLM says it's the same as it always was, good as it used to be. Think the natives don't know nothin'. Some guys who read it all out of a book, no practical experience, tellin' ya it's the same as it used to be."

On the future: "Unless someone does somethin' about the water—like plans for

Overleaf: *The Ekker ranch after the first snowfall of the year.*

Belle Starr left a trail of blood behind her.
After a lifetime of horse thievery she was
finally shot to death.

irrigation usin' the Green or Colorado River, I guess coal is the way they'll go. Land will be taken over by the Park Service and the BLM and we'll have to leave. Coal will bring a lot of people. Won't be more sheep, no way for livestock to thrive."

I mentioned that new technologies were being developed for growing crops and food in areas of the desert and perhaps such technologies could be applied to this area. Ekker looked at me and said, "Yeah, but that'd take a lot of money, wouldn't it?"

Nighttime settled in like a great welcome blanket to a beautiful day. All tension was gone and fatigue was wholesome and welcome.

he next day we rode out of the Roost. I rode along with A.C. (who likes to talk while trotting; my voice tends to get caught between my teeth) and he told me about the "tenderfoot syndrome."

"We took a bunch of hunters down to Horse Thief Canyon. It's a steep canyon but they said they wanted to go. One of the boys panicked and two horses went over the side with guitars, whiskey, sleepin' bags. I jumped off and a mule stepped right over me—didn't want no part of it. What a mess it was. Thing you have to watch for is these tenderfoot panickin'."

I said he must get sick and tired taking out hunters who want to shoot elk and such, and then complain about the rough conditions.

"Yeah, they're a problem. Ya know, when they start out in the mornin' they're tough, then in an hour or two they're done. That's what's disgustin'. Travelin' over rock is tricky. Horse can fall real easy.

This man, known only as Blue Duck, was Belle Starr's boyfriend.

Got to know how to go."

I asked him if he'd seen any cow mutilation in the area.

"Yeah, a few cows round here. Up on the Range Valley Mountains just recently, for example—high peaks around, no way to get in there. Mom's brother lost a lot of cows. Funny thing though, crows wouldn't go near the dead animals even after they decayed. Can't figure it. Some say its helicopters."

A. C. Ekker is a man of unusual efficiency. He's a take-charge man, impatient with lethargy and complication. He is simple, in the best sense of the word, and has an extraordinary ability to see a task clearly and reduce its complications to the simplest level. This I admire.

"Well, I'd love it, of course, if ranchin' was a bit like it used to be, but you can't make it on cows now so I'd bet that workin' this river-trip-backpack-trail-ride business is where it'll be."

I mentioned that the shrinking livestock business had been the constant complaint we'd heard all during our trail ride.

"Well, you see, the rancher today can't compete with the beef they're importin' from Argentina and Venezuela. They raise lean beef there from smaller cows bred specially for the job, and that lean beef is what supplies most all of the fast-food chains in this country. So imports are dominatin' our trade and cuttin' into our market. And with the current recession, feed prices are up so high and sale prices so low that we end up losin'. Because of Earl Butz [then Secretary of Agriculture] everything we do today is tied to foreign policy, so we're busy scratchin' everybody's back abroad, and we're out."

I thought how refreshing someone like Ekker might be in Washington.

GLEN CANYON

We were headed south now, out of the Roost, down across Dirty Devil River past Hanksville to Halls Crossing, which is a marina on the east end of Lake Powell. Here we had arranged to leave our horses behind and navigate the next-to-last section of our ride by boat. This would permit us to float up some of the canyons that held great historical detail, while being in touch with the textures that define the awesome beauty of this unusual area. Lake Powell is the dammed-up section of the lower Colorado River. Some two hundred miles long, with a labyrinth of fingers and tributaries, it has more shoreline than the entire coast of California. Defined by Ed Abbey in his book *Desert Solitaire* as slick rock country, this almost prehistoric wonderland is little known to most Americans since the foraging of progress and development has scarcely grazed it. Great chasms of rock, sometimes eight hundred feet high, were covered by the damming of the river, as were most of the ruins, artifacts, petroglyphs and pictographs of the Anasazi Indians, the earliest known inhabitants of this part of the West who predate the Pueblo.

The prehistoric stone arches of Lake Powell in early morning sunlight.

These early basket makers were descendants of the hunting and gathering people who supposedly migrated across the Bering Strait from Siberia and headed south into this region. Those that settled here took up a sedentary life dependent on agriculture, while the more warlike tribes moved on. These early Indians were peaceful themselves but needed fortification against invading tribes, so they carved their dwellings high in the Navajo sandstone cliffs above the Colorado River where they had a view of every access from below. Their dwellings were usually carved out of concave rock so they were protected from invasion from above as well. The Anasazi were the ancestors of the Pueblo tribes that settled in the famous Mesa Verde in Colorado around A.D. 700. The Mesa Verde civilization thrived for about six hundred years, marked by great advances in basket weaving and pottery. Then around A.D. 1300 it suddenly disappeared, possibly as a result of a drought that is known to have lasted for thirty years.

Halls Crossing is a small oasis in a desert of mirages like something one comes upon unexpectedly after resigning oneself to dying of exposure or lost bearings. In 1870 a man named Hall established the first ferry service across the four-mile stretch to the west side of the river. This enabled explorers, prospectors, miners, outlaws and Indians to gain access to the east or west in quick time. Not much has changed since then. Halls Crossing today is a beautiful marina set against two large bullfrog rocks that act as sentinels to the channel below. When we arrived, the sun was going down over prehistoric stone formations. And again those purple mountains. (The color in the Utah mountains at sunset is *definitely* purple.) The clouds, boiling up like geothermal steam over the Henry Mountains, were red-lined from the reflection of the clay. The warmth of the sun on the snow peaks was condensing into vaporous pillows and the whole sight was one to freeze in time. I had never had so many extraordinary visual experiences in so short a time. Or was it that I had never paid as much attention before?

We loaded supplies onto the rented boat, a sort of Noah's Ark of good will, and arranged with A. C. Ekker to take the horses down around the lake by land and meet us above Page, Arizona. We would cover the last miles on horseback.

We headed down the main channel of the lake in search of a campsite for the night. We were pressed for time since winter light dies fast and the canyon beauty can turn into a nightmare within minutes. Now we were in territory where I could act as guide. I have spent much time in the last ten years in these rocks and canyons and on this river. The impressive, quiet, voluptuous rock formations and almost spooky quiet draw me like a magnet. I was eager to share the virtues of this land I love with the group.

I wanted to reach a spot called Davis Gulch, one of the many veins that meander off the main stem of the Escalante River, itself a spectacular tributary that runs north for forty miles off the main Lake Powell channel. It is here that many outdoor survival trips are conducted; it is a place to truly test one's capabilities in parched country.

The river was named for Father Escalante, a Dominican priest who was one of the early explorers of this region and the architect of the famous Escalante Trail. This trail was a main lateral traverse in early days of pioneering.

Davis Gulch is a narrow and winding tributary so one must weave through it as though threading a needle. It is beautiful—and dangerous, as beautiful things often are—and culminates in a magnificent concave stone shield, an amphitheater of carved rock, festooned with early Indian pictographs. I carefully navigated our boat through familiar channels, remembering other moments when under similar conditions lives and property had been endangered, thinking how close I had come to disaster on so many occasions. How lucky to have come through and learned from it. As Ed Abbey said, "You really learn something

These pictographs (below) drawn by the Anasazi Indians decorate the stone walls of Davis Gulch (opposite), a winding tributary of Lake Powell.

by having panicked over it at least once.

In an atmosphere of combustible silence we finally pulled safely into the camp area. The elevated sand platform at the base of the rock was just a shadow in the early night. We quickly built a fire from driftwood collected along the way, and soon the fire was reflecting and bouncing off the walls of the open cave and the warmth returned to everyone's tongue. There was a bit of that manic behavior that accompanies relief—similar to chatting your seat partner's head off after a near plane crash.

Later, after cooking some bass caught near the marina, everyone soon mellowed into

Jesse James had his first taste of killing fighting for the Confederacy during the Civil War. One year after the war, he and his older brother Frank along with the Younger brothers participated in one of the first bank robberies in the nation's history. After a lifetime of thievery and violence, Jesse was shot in the back by Bob Ford (right), a member of the James gang.

reflection. I was struck by the frequency of this reaction as the trail ride progressed; it was developing into a pattern. The surprising thing was that we had all become so compatible and it was in this sense an unusual group. Everyone seemed to give way to others' needs and the territorial imperative didn't apply here. To have lived so closely and on such intimate terms for the length of time we had been riding, and not have at least one major fallout, seemed impossible. But so it had been. I suspect the experience was so new and overpowering in its infinite variety that we were all somewhat awed.

Then out of the silence that precedes dozing-off came a surprise. Out of nowhere came the incredible sound of a flute. It was Ed Abbey. No one knew he could play the flute let alone carried one with him. It was a sound both pleasing and powerful, pure and simple and oddly so right for the setting.

In the next morning's light cool arches of stone stood in perfect symmetry—such large volumes of space, calm and solid. Breakfast was prepared against this magical backdrop

Winnemucca, Nevada in 1885. Bill Carver, Butch Cassidy, and the Sundance Kid held up the bank in this town to finance their trip to South America.

of Indian paintings, the sensuous rock forms, the still water not yet ruffled by the day's sun. It was a setting where one might reach for a camera, or a notepad, but didn't.

We traveled on down to the southern end of our journey, passing through ruins and landmarks in a kaleidoscopic blur, coming upon "The Crossing of the Father" and Hole-in-the-Rock where the early Mormons on their trek to the southeastern part of Utah had endured great hardships while crossing the river with wagons, animals and supplies. This niche, some five hundred feet up in the

cliffs, stands as a reminder of their fortitude and will. Here in 1879, over a period of months, they carved steps in the rock and dismantled their wagons and lowered all the animals and wagon parts by rope and pulley to the river, where the parts were assembled into rafts used to float the party across. The spot reminded me a great deal of Hole-in-the-Wall in Wyoming.

At one point we attempted to pass through a narrow crevice in a rock that would take us from one finger of the lake to the next, where there were some old rock carvings done by

the early outlaws and miners. It was decided that to save time someone would bring the boat around to meet us. During the climb through the crevice we had to cross over a waterway below us by employing a technique known as "chimneying." You keep your weight balanced and suspended over a space by applying pressure to either side of the space you are straddling. Those who weren't used to it or had never done it were understandably apprehensive at the substantial drop to the water below. Once one of us had made it to the other side, we hooked my belt and Ed Abbey's together as a lifeline to help the others. It was tricky and fun and the best of it was having to use some ingenuity.

We reached the end of our river journey by mid-afternoon and joined forces with the dependable A. C. Ekker and one of his ranch hands. Then we saddled up once again and proceeded south toward Page, Arizona.

Page is something of a cultural hybrid, like Rock Springs and Gillette, Wyoming. It is a community mostly of people who work in the nearby Navajo Power Plant, a large mechanized anomaly in this otherwise stark landscape. It is axiomatic today that energy creates jobs and the power plant and the neighboring community of Page are perfect illustrations of this point.

In the fifties, when construction on the Lake Powell Dam was completed, most of the portable work force moved on to other construction jobs. Before that, during the great boom-town expansion at the turn of the century, people in tents and covered wagons were mining here for the "material grail."

Ironically, the power produced here on the edge of Navajo Indian reservation land goes to California, since the plant is the brainchild of Southern California Edison. Leaving time and history to decide the merits of this development, one thing is certain: it doesn't fit. It is aesthetically a rude imposition on an otherwise awesome sight of space and color that has prehistoric dimensions. As we rode on horseback in front of the plant with its sci-fi strobe lights atop four hundred-foot towers and its wide corridor of transmission lines stretching fourteen hundred miles to California, I felt like an anachronism. So it goes, times change. They say we can't have it both ways and maybe we can't. There is talk of an even larger plant (the largest in the United States) going in across the lake on the Utah side. So it goes.

It seemed only fitting that we finish our trail ride at the home in which Butch Cassidy grew up, and celebrate with a visit to Butch's sister, Lula Betenson, who is in her nineties and lives in the nearby town of Circleville. This would complete the story, although the actual trail did not end here. In fact, at this point the trail divided into many arteries leading east, west and south.

Lula Betenson and I had first met in the fall of 1968 when she visited the set while we were filming *Butch Cassidy and the*

Ed Abbey.

Overleaf: *The gargantuan form of the Navajo Power Plant appears against the Arizona landscape.*

This 1906 photograph was taken inside the Alred & Hudson Bar, Alma, New Mexico. Left to right: Charley Hudson, Bronson McMahon, Wes Ford, George Graham, Jasper Hudson, Brad Hudson, and John Alred.

Ben Thompson.

Sundance Kid. She struck me then as an unusual person, spry, witty, strong-willed, with a gentle feminine spirit that warmed you. Since that time we have become friends and I try to visit her at least once a year. She taught me how to make sourdough bread.

Lula, one of thirteen children, was six years old when Butch left home, but she has saved his letters and personal belongings all these years. To this day she stays in touch with all the surviving relatives of the Wild Bunch by letters and visits. (She had just been over to Heber, Utah, to see Marvel

Overleaf: Power lines outside Page, Arizona,
suggest a new type of trail emerging in the West.

Murdoch, Elza Lay's daughter.) She now lives with one of her sons, Mark.

As we pulled in at the white frame house at the end of a dirt road, we were warmly greeted. I was struck by Lula's beauty, even at this age. She is tall and elegant, a proud person who enjoys living.

Wearing a black dress trimmed in powder blue and pink, a pink sweater over her shoulders, Lula took us into her sitting room. Always energetic, she jumped up from time to time to get someone coffee or whatever,

This reward poster issued by the Pinkerton Agency reveals the increasing amount of information in their files on the Wild Bunch.

Silver City, New Mexico, the home of Billy the Kid. This photograph is dated 1872.

refusing to let any of us do anything. She talked about how much mail she'd been getting (the letters come from as far away as London), and how she loves it and fills her days responding. Then she asked us why we all moved around so much, what the rush was, and said she hoped we were all getting something out of it.

Later Mark led us out to the original homestead and the cabin where Butch and Lula grew up. Judging from early pictures of Butch (mostly on wanted posters), Mark resembles his uncle with his square jaw, wide mouth and blue eyes. Mark, who smiles often, has the same raucous energy that gave Butch the reputation of being affable and fun-loving, a man who seemed to fight being robbed of his childhood by time.

It was late afternoon and a light autumn breeze was blowing leaves around the cabin.

At the old Parker cabin near Circleville, Utah the author visits with Butch Cassidy's sister, ninety-four-year-old Lula Parker Betenson.

Lula and I walked off together through the old house and around the land. She told me she had lost her sight in one eye and was starting to lose it in the other. She feared that blindness might bring loss of her real spirit. She took hold of my arm and looked at me straight on.

"I'm fightin' the melancholy," she said. "Don't like good-byes . . . can't stand 'em. Never used to bother me." She pointed to the walls of the cabin inside. "Mother and I used to whitewash the walls and cover the ceiling with fabric for the winter. Sometimes the Indians would come through unexpected, and I'd hide. Sometimes they were drunk."

She seemed cameo-locket pretty standing there in the late afternoon sun framed by the cottonwood trees and the old cabin. Such a youthful countenance with young eyes, pleading not to be covered by the mask of old age. Her mind is thirty years or more younger and her desire is as strong as a young girl's. How had she lived so long?

"I don't overeat. I don't eat meat, I eat lots of grains and I stay busy."

The house is old. Gray-splintered sagging wood. The window frames are bleached and vandalism and target practice have left smashed panes. The rooms are small, like all the rooms in all the buildings of this kind we have visited. In the back are the corrals—gray, shaggy, tilting against the burnt yellow and gray hills beyond.

It's all that's left. Lula and the corrals and the hills. There's no more.

INDEX

PHOTO CREDITS